## "What are you thinking about?"

Why, Ben wondered, did her radar always zero in on him when he least wanted it to?

He hesitated. It wasn't likely that he could put his conflicting thoughts into a coherent explanation even if he wanted to. Frankie remained silent, sipping her own coffee and looking away from him.

Finally he answered, "I'm thinking about Dad and wondering what I should do."

Frankie did look at him then, and her eyes— beautiful eyes, Ben thought, not for the first time—were filled with understanding.

"Maybe I can help?" she offered. "I mean, I can't make the decision for you, but I've observed a lot of seniors and I've seen what their families go through. It might help even to just talk about it."

"It might," Ben conceded. But he stayed silent. And while it was true that his thoughts were always edged with worry about his father, he was also trying to comprehend the mixture of traits—hard and defensive, soft and empathetic—that composed his summer neighbor.

**Donna Gartshore** loves reading and writing. She also writes short stories, poetry and devotionals. She often veers off to the book section in the grocery store when she should be buying food. Besides talking about books and writing, Donna loves spending time with her daughter, Sunday family suppers and engaging online with the writing community.

### Books by Donna Gartshore

### Love Inspired

*Instant Family*

# Instant Family

## Donna Gartshore

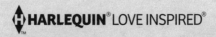
HARLEQUIN® LOVE INSPIRED®

Recycling programs for this product may not exist in your area.

LOVE INSPIRED BOOKS

ISBN-13: 978-1-335-42785-4

Instant Family

Copyright © 2017 by Donna Lynn Gartshore

www.Harlequin.com

**Printed in U.S.A.**

Trust in the Lord with all thine heart;
and lean not unto thine own understanding.
In all thy ways acknowledge Him,
and He shall direct thy paths.
—*Proverbs* 3:5–6

This book is dedicated in memory of my father,
Ian Franklin Bickle, and my husband,
James Douglas Gartshore.

And it is for Sara Gartshore, who has made
every single day of being her mom a blessing,
and for my family, near and far, who mean more
to me than I can express.

Thanks also to my wonderful editor,
Melissa Endlich, for giving me this chance.

# Chapter One

"Is this the surprise you talked about, Mom?"

Somewhere in her mind, Frankie Munro registered her daughter's tremulous question and felt Rae's small, sweaty hand clutching her own. But she couldn't find the words to answer her.

A surprise, indeed, but not a pleasant one and not at all the one she had been planning to share.

The cabin that she had booked for the summer was covered in violent-looking splashes of paint and offensive graffiti. In no way did it represent the rustic yet pristine atmosphere she had pored over in the brochures advertising Silver Lake Park in Saskatchewan, Canada. It had been a six-hour drive from their home in Regina, Saskatchewan, and they had passed the time talking of the possibility of bear sightings with a kind of gleeful fear, and speculating how cold the water would be.

Since Frankie's husband walked out on them several months ago, she wanted to do something to return the light to Rae's eyes. Rae was an intuitive ten-year-old with an advanced talent for art, but it had been months since Frankie had seen her enthusiastic about drawing or painting. She hoped that spending the summer together, away from their house and the memories it held, would help return a spark of artistic interest to Rae, and with that would come a return to the happy, inquisitive girl she had been.

She hoped the time away would help restore some of her own motivation, too. She'd had goals—she wanted to be a nurse—and although those goals had been put on the back burner due to her ex-husband's demands, they still simmered within her. Frankie wanted to use the summer to rediscover the woman she had been before Trevor left: the woman who'd had goals…the woman who'd had faith.

Frankie worked as a nurse's aide at a senior-care home in Regina. She usually liked her job very much and had a true affinity for the seniors she worked with. But in the months after her husband left, she'd been a mass of nerves, mistakes and indecisions, until the manager of the home had called her in and explained that she had to take some time off and find an effective way to deal with her obvious stress.

Thus, a paid leave of absence, combined with financial help from her parents, which Frankie had accepted only after they signed a note saying she would pay them back in full as soon as she could, cleared the pathway for her to plan this summer getaway with Rae.

Research and word of mouth had brought her to the conclusion that Silver Lake looked like a positive place with the right balance of nature and town activities. The beautifully scenic photographs of trees, flowers and local animals gave her hope that Rae would feel compelled to capture them on canvas. As the plans came together, her hope for a new start began to grow tentatively. She had not yet decided if that new start would include a church.

But now, as they looked at the vandalized cabin, Frankie prayed silently, an ache of regret in her throat. *God, I wanted You to meet us here.*

Suddenly, rapid footsteps came up behind them and Frankie spun quickly around. The man approaching them was very handsome. He was also very angry.

"What are you doing?" the stranger demanded. His dark blue eyes seemed to give off sparks of fury. "Why are you lurking around these cabins?"

Frankie attempted to give Rae a reassuring smile and stepped in front of her, adopting a defensive stance. Not that she thought she had any real hope of intimidating this stranger, since she stood at five foot four and he had to be at least six feet tall. Still, if he imagined he was going to threaten them or get anywhere near her daughter, she'd do whatever she could to prove him wrong.

"We're not lurking," Frankie told him, hoping that if she spoke loudly enough it would mask the way her voice was shaking. "I paid to rent this cabin and we get here and—this!" Her hand flipped toward the vandalized cabin with a gesture that managed to be both defiant and defeated.

The man studied them with a speculative look on his face, then relaxed his shoulders and stepped back.

Ben Cedar felt decidedly chagrined. He had thought the small, slight figure wearing cutoff shorts, a T-shirt and a baseball cap was a teenage boy, with his little sister, but he'd already launched into his tirade before he realized his mistake.

This woman, whoever she was, might be dressed in a boyish fashion, but up close she was unmistakably female. He didn't think he'd ever seen skin quite as smooth and golden peachy or features so delicate. He could see the sheer resilience it took for her to keep her brown eyes locked to his. Behind her, the girl peeked out, her eyes wide and her hands over her mouth.

Ben felt even worse and tried to give the little girl a friendly smile, but she gave an audible gasp and retreated.

The woman looked like she would take great pleasure in maiming him or worse.

"I'm sorry," he said, attempting to rectify the situation. "I didn't mean to frighten you." He tried to push out another smile, but the truth was that he didn't need any more complications added to his summer—or to his life—and he just wanted the misunderstanding to go away as quickly as possible.

The woman didn't answer, but her expression clearly said that he wasn't convincing her.

"My name's Ben Cedar," he said, making another attempt. "My father and I are here for the summer. We've spent every summer here since I was a kid. My mom used to…" He stopped himself and said more briskly, "Well, anyway, yours isn't the only cabin to be vandalized. It's been happening all over the place and some of the town businesses have been hit, too. It's really put a damper on people's vacations." Regret darkened his eyes. "It's a real shame, too," he said. "This has always been such a great place for families. I have a lot of happy memories here. I don't know what's gone wrong, though I have some suspicions."

"Well, I'm sorry to hear that, but my daughter and I don't appreciate being accused," the woman said. Despite the slight tremor in her voice, her stiff posture and rigid mouth told Ben that she wasn't about to concede her ground easily.

*Lord, please help me make this right.*

"Hello, there!" said another voice.

Ben closed his eyes for a moment, feeling a pulse of anxiety. Now was definitely not the time for his father to make a scene. He silently reminded himself to be patient. His dad couldn't help his behavior and, besides, having one last memorable summer with him was one of the main reasons that Ben was here.

Ben thought about what was facing him at summer's end, and an acute ache pulsed behind his eyes. But he couldn't dwell on that now. The time to move his father into full-time care loomed soon enough without him letting his worry about it devour the days they had here.

His father grinned and waved happily at the little girl, and Ben braced himself.

"Would you like to walk down to the beach with me and look for seashells?" he asked her, as if it were the most natural thing in the world for him to say to a little girl he had never met.

Ben saw the woman study his father for a moment, and then a glimmer of understanding crept into her eyes.

"Dad, we don't know these people," he said, willing a gentle voice, almost as if speaking to a child. "And you know what I've told you about talking to strangers."

The man hung his head and shuffled his feet back and forth in the dirt on the road between the cabins. The action stirred up a small cloud of dust.

"Did you have your nap?" Ben asked.

His dad shrugged and his open face threatened to collapse into a scowl.

Ben pretended not to notice the change in his dad's mood and pushed away the foreboding in his own gut. It was, he reminded himself, the least he could do to take care of his father. Especially since there were times that he hadn't been there when he should have been.

"You know I told you that if you had a nap and gave me some time to get some things done, I would take you for ice cream," Ben said, pushing down the surge of guilt that threatened to rise up into his throat. The last thing he needed was to feel more guilt over this woman and girl he didn't even know.

The man's mouth made shapes without any

words coming out and he kicked the dirt harder, in an expression of inarticulate frustration.

"Mom?" The girl tugged on her mother's hand and whispered loudly, "What's wrong with that man?"

"Rae…" the woman began to protest.

"It's okay," Ben said, directing his words to her. "My father has Alzheimer's disease. I'm not sure how to explain that to your little girl."

Her lovely brown eyes searched his face for a moment and then she gave a small nod. She glanced down at the girl.

"I'll explain later, Rae." She looked at Ben again. "Any ideas on what I can do about the cabin?"

"If you can wait until I get my dad settled again, I'll take you down to the office and you can talk to the people who manage these cabins."

"Will they be able to do anything about it? I think I should go talk to them right away."

"They've been getting cleaning crews out. If you can hold off just a bit, it might help if I go with you. They've known Dad and me for a long time."

Ben's father started to wander off and Ben reached out and took his hand. They tussled briefly as the older man tried to get away, but eventually he calmed down and allowed his son to lead him back toward their cabin.

"There's a good place for ice cream just at the end of the walk," Ben said over his shoulder. "Turn right. It's the place with all the big umbrellas."

After a challenging ten minutes or so, Ben got his father settled back into their cabin and gave him a pile of hand towels to fold to keep him preoccupied. He found that repetitive activities calmed his father.

Ben eased himself out the cabin door, locking it behind him. He walked quickly, then broke into a jog, anxious to get to the Ice Cream Adventure as soon as possible. He had to admit that it wasn't only because he was worried about what his Dad might do if he got bored of folding and realized that he had been left alone in the cabin. He told himself that he just wanted to get the situation rectified as quickly as possible. But something about the woman—her fragility, combined with her obvious determination to be strong—tugged at him.

When he spotted them sitting under a gaudy orange umbrella, nibbling and licking at ice-cream cones, Ben breathed a thankful prayer.

He paused a moment to gather himself. He'd already made a bad first impression and he didn't want to swoop down on them like he was on a hunt.

"Hi," he said, as he drew near to their table. "I see you waited."

The woman studied him as if she was trying to decide what would be an appropriate response. Ben noticed how long her eyelashes were, framing her large, expressive eyes.

Finally, she said, "Well, there wasn't really much else we could do, was there?" She looked at her little girl to signify she didn't want to alarm her any more than she had been.

Her tone was mild enough, but it made Ben squirm a little.

"I'd really like it if we could start fresh," he said. "So, when you're finished your ice cream, I'd be happy to go with you to the office to explain the situation and make sure you get the help you need."

The last part of his statement made the woman suddenly sit up straight in her chair and square her shoulders.

"Thank you for your concern," she said in a polite tone with frosted tips, "but I'll figure something out."

The little girl nibbled her ice-cream cone like a nervous mouse and her eyes darted up to Ben, back to her mother and back to Ben again.

"Look," Ben said, "I know it was wrong of

me to take my stress out on you, but can you please forgive me so we can move past it?"

Was it his imagination, or did her mouth stiffen a bit at the word *forgive*?

She shrugged. "Okay, no big deal. We all have stress, right?"

Ben found himself wanting to ask her what she was stressed about. *You don't need to know,* he reminded himself. *You have enough of your own to deal with right now.*

These days, it felt like it was nothing more than sheer effort, coupled with a long-standing faith, that kept him from wondering why he bothered with God. Yet, although his father's disease now challenged Ben, it was his father who had taught him in the first place to trust God in all situations.

*The tough times are when you have to lean on him harder than ever,* his father had always said.

*Lord, I'm leaning as hard as I can. Please help me to trust that You won't let me fall.*

He shook himself out of his reverie and realized that the child was watching him warily.

She was a cute little girl, he thought, although a bit unkempt, with the ends of her braids going fuzzy in the humidity and her glasses sitting a bit lopsided on her nose. He also noted that she must take after her father, wherever he was, because her features were round and soft, whereas her mother's features were small and delicate. Regardless, he certainly wasn't going to ask.

"I won't force my help on you," Ben said, looking from one to another, "but please let me know if you need anything. Since we're going to be neighbors for the summer, I hope we can get along. I'm Ben Cedar."

The woman scrutinized his face again. Ben wished he could ask her what she was looking for, although he sensed that she might not be able to answer that question even if she wanted to. Then she gave a brief sharp nod as if she'd made a decision.

"Frankie," she said. "And my daughter is Rae."

"Nice to meet you," Ben said. He noticed that ice cream from Frankie's cone was melting its sweet and sticky way down her arm while she kept her eyes on him.

He looked away. Something told him she wouldn't appreciate it being pointed out to her.

"Frankie?" he said, instead. "Is that a nickname for something? Frances? Or Francesca?"

"Francesca," she repeated with a little snort of laughter that surprised him. "Um, no. I'm not exactly the Francesca type. My Mom's favorite book is *The Member of the Wedding*, but I doubt you've heard of it."

"I remember there was an old movie," Ben replied. "Julie Harris, right?"

He felt a certain degree of satisfaction when Frankie blinked her surprise.

"I watched it with my dad one night," he said. "It was on the late show, some channel where they play old movies."

Mentioning his dad brought a rush of trepidation to Ben. He really had to get back to the cabin.

Frankie noticed her arm and, with a quick, somewhat accusing glance in his direction, began to wipe the ice cream off with a napkin.

"Are you done?" she said to Rae. "We'd better go see someone about our cabin. It's going to be fine," she hurried to reassure her daughter, who suddenly looked like a wizened and worried little old woman. "It's going to be just fine. I promise."

Ben thought that the little girl would have no idea what it cost her mother to make that promise, and he could see the sheer will it took for Frankie to keep a smile on her face for the sake of her daughter.

He made a decision then and sent a quick prayer up to the Lord daring to ask Him to bless what was quite possibly the most inane idea he'd ever had. Still, if it would fix the problem and let him get his focus back on why this summer was so important to him—the amends he needed to make—he was willing to take the chance.

"I have a great idea. You'll take our cabin," he said, hoping he sounded more confident than he felt, "and we'll move into yours." He wondered how he would get his father and their belongings relocated. But the words were out and there was no way he was taking them back.

"If you can just find something to do for another hour or so, I'll stop into the office and make all the arrangements."

"I need to let them know I'm here," Frankie protested.

Ben braced himself to stand his ground.

"Could we please, Mom?" Rae's small voice floated up like a hopeful balloon between them. "I really want a nice cabin like you promised."

"Please let me do this," Ben said, nodding his head toward Rae. "I can explain everything to them and you and your daughter can just relax for a bit, and then we'll call it even."

"Even?" Frankie retorted. "What have I done for you?"

"You'll be doing something for me by *letting* me make up for the misunderstanding," Ben said.

Frankie held Rae's hands as they took their time looking at the displays in the Nature Center. At least Rae looked, and Frankie was grateful that her daughter was occupied. It gave her time to try to organize her own thoughts, which had been jumping from place to place like a skittish cat since they had first laid eyes on their vandalized cabin.

First and foremost, she absolutely had to make sure this summer was a healing time for Rae. As well, she had come to Silver Lake seeking to regain and strengthen her own independence, so she was not happy about needing help from a stranger almost from their first moment there. She hadn't even wanted to accept financial help from her own parents. When she had heard Ben say that the beach community had been plagued with vandalism this summer, she had fought hard against the feeling that her goals for the summer would fail.

Frankie's thoughts jumped to Ben. She wasn't at all sure what to think of him, and at the same time asked herself why she should bother thinking about him at all.

Yet, even if his physical appeal wasn't enough to draw her attention, there was a complexity about him that intrigued her more than she wanted to admit. He was apologetic and polite on the surface, though she sensed that something darker simmered beneath, as if he had plenty of his own troubles—or secrets—to worry about… Still, his concern and gentleness with his father was evident, and he had insisted on giving up his cabin for them, people he didn't even know. What kind of person did something like that?

She felt an impatient yank on her hand, which meant Rae had been trying to get her attention.

"Look!" Rae said. "There's that man again."

Had Ben come to find them? Frankie wondered.

But, no, the man who ambled with a shuffling gait among the displays, poking out his finger to touch the stuffed and mounted animals, was Ben's father.

## Chapter Two

Frankie wondered anxiously if she should approach him. Although she knew he shouldn't be unattended, she had no idea how he would react to her. Where was Ben? Still, she had worked as an aide in a senior-care home since Rae was six, and almost by instinct she found herself moving toward Ben's father.

Just before she reached him, a plump woman sporting a large name tag that proclaimed her as a Nature Center volunteer, stepped between them and said rather officiously, "Please don't touch the displays, sir."

Ben's father weaved his head a bit like he was trying to focus on a faraway noise, and then he gave the standing bear, with its ferocious grimace, a little pat.

"I said don't touch, sir!" the volunteer said more sharply. "Please step away!"

Ben's father looked confused and his tongue darted out the corner of his mouth. Suddenly Frankie had that swell of feeling she sometimes got at the care home—the one when she didn't know whether to laugh or cry.

In another moment, though, any inclination to laugh was shoved aside abruptly.

The volunteer reached out and clasped his forearm.

Ben's father's eyes widened in shock and rage; his mouth flew open and a horrible cry came out of it. Then he shoved her with all of his might, causing her to lose her balance, stagger back a few steps and topple a display of pert-looking chipmunks.

Even before she could get to her feet, the volunteer was fumbling for her phone as she threatened to call Security.

Frankie's eyes darted around and found Rae, who looked utterly stricken. She tried to smile reassuringly at her, but felt torn between going to soothe her daughter and staying to help Ben's father.

Rae would have to understand, Frankie told herself. If she saw her mother being strong and helping someone when it was the right thing to do, it would benefit both of them.

The other patrons at the Nature Center had drifted awkwardly away from the scene, although, Frankie noted with wryness, they stayed close enough to see how things were going to unfold. She headed toward Ben's father to offer assistance.

"Dad!" Ben's voice drew her attention. He hurried toward them with a look of relief seasoned with a dash of frustration.

"Dad, I'm so glad you're safe." Temporarily unmindful of the chaos around him, Ben put his hands on his father's shoulders and looked into his eyes before drawing him into a hug.

His flare of violent temper gone, Ben's father subsided into his son's arms like a docile child.

"I like animals," he said softly.

"I know you do, Dad. I know. But you have to wait for me to bring you here. You can't just disappear on me."

While Ben spoke patiently to his father, Frankie watched a slight pulse at the corner of his eye that indicated how stressful the incident had been for him.

"So, I assume you're the one responsible for this—this gentleman?" The volunteer had struggled to her feet and directed her question to Ben.

"He's my father," Ben replied. "Most folks know us around here," he said, attempting to be friendly and smooth things over. "So, I take it you're new? How long have—"

"Well, I suggest you keep him under control," she said, "before he hurts someone else."

"He didn't mean to hurt you," Ben said. "He's just…"

"He's crazy is what he is!"

Something flared in Frankie and she stepped forward.

"These gentlemen happen to be very good friends of mine," she declared. "And I can assure you that he's about the furthest thing from crazy that you could ever want! Perhaps you need to work on how you approach your visitors so that you don't offend them."

She looked at Ben, whose befuddled expression would have made her giggle under different circumstances. Obviously, nothing in their brief acquaintance would have prepared him for the declaration that they were close friends. Fortunately, the volunteer's focus wasn't on him at the moment.

"Let's go," Frankie said to Ben and his father, who clung to his son's hand and studied his feet. "Come on, Rae, we're going back to the cabins."

Rae chewed her lip, a sign that she was very puzzled. But she took her mother's hand and the four of them left together.

Once outside, Ben held his father by the hand and hurried up beside Frankie and murmured,

"I suppose I should say thank you, but would you mind telling me what that was all about?"

"I work with seniors," she said, "and I knew your dad needed help. Besides, I hate labels like that."

"Like 'crazy'?"

She nodded.

They walked together for a little while, not saying anything.

Frankie took in the eclectic shops ranging from a hairdresser to a sporting-goods store to a small art gallery. She loved the smell of the air and seeing the tall pine trees.

"My dad used to be a minister," Ben offered quietly. "He was one of the kindest, wisest men you'd ever want to meet." Sadness and another expression that Frankie couldn't quite decipher flickered across his face.

Ben's father had let go of his hand and walked beside Rae, slightly in front of them. "I'm Al," Frankie heard him tell Rae. "Who are you?"

Frankie wasn't sure how Rae would react, both because of the unusual situation and because she had become much more reticent since her dad had left. But she just looked shyly up at Al and shuffled her feet a bit. "I'm Rae," she told him.

The two of them continued to stroll together in what looked like a compatible silence.

Rae was an intuitive little girl, and she could probably sense that Al didn't mean any harm, despite what she had seen at the Nature Center.

She also noticed Ben's stiff shoulders loosen slightly. His handsome face no longer looked as agitated as it had, but still wore deep shadows of the devastating kind of fatigue she knew could overcome long-term caregivers: the kind of fatigue people had when they knew things would only get worse.

"What about your mother?" Frankie asked. "Do you have any brothers or sisters to help out?" She avoided asking him why he hadn't placed his father in permanent care. She knew that the decision to do so was very complex, colored by each family's experiences and emotions.

She also wasn't going to ask if he was married and why his wife wasn't with him if he was. It was none of her business and she certainly didn't care. She had noticed that he wasn't wearing a ring, but these days that didn't mean anything.

"Mom died two years ago," Ben said. "Ovarian cancer."

"I'm so sorry. It's horrible watching someone go through that."

"I was away," Ben said tersely, in a tone that clearly indicated he wanted no further questions. He reached up and brushed his hair off his forehead. Frankie found herself wondering why she'd never been attracted to a man with light hair before. Trevor's hair had been dark.

"Is something the matter?" Ben asked, catching her gaze.

Frankie felt her cheeks flush. "No," she said shortly.

After another moment, he said quietly. "I'm glad Mom never had to see Dad like this."

She nodded. She understood there was nothing to say.

"As for your other question, I'm an only child so it's just Dad and me now."

"It's just Rae and me," Frankie heard herself say, and inwardly cringed a little. She didn't tell people personal things about herself, especially men. She just didn't. She rapidly changed the subject. "I'm sure your dad appreciates you, even if he can't always tell you."

For a moment weariness and something darker shadowed Ben's features.

"It's the least I can do," he said.

He glanced over at Al and Rae and said, "Is your daughter okay with him, do you think? I don't want her to be uncomfortable."

Throughout her conversation with Ben, Frankie had been able to hear the light, gentle notes of her daughter's voice, telling Al that she liked Sunday school and that she was allergic to peanuts.

"She's doing fine," she said, and was pleasantly surprised herself. Maybe Rae paid more attention than Frankie thought when she talked about her work and how important it was to treat seniors with dignity.

"Anyway," Ben said, "before Dad wandered off, we did go to the office and I got everything straightened out. I asked Paula—she's the manager—to open the cabin and, thankfully, there isn't any damage to the inside. Dad and I are fine to stay there and they'll get cleanup crews for the outside damage as soon as they can. Our cabin is clean for you."

"You didn't have to do that," Frankie said again.

"It's already done." His tone brooked no argument.

Well, Frankie reasoned to herself, she could accept it for Rae's sake. Even if the inside of the cabin was fine, she knew it wouldn't feel right to sleep in a cabin that had been vandalized whether for reasons of mischief or true malice.

"You said there'd been vandalism around here," she said. "Do you think it's safe for us to stay here?" Her head began to drum out an ache and her nerves to strum an accompaniment as she thought of her parents' generosity and the promises she had made to Rae. Ben appeared to give his answer careful consideration.

"It's disturbing," he said, "and it's getting very expensive for the town—all the cleaning supplies and fresh paint. But I honestly don't think anyone is in any danger."

Frankie nodded, pondering.

"Does anyone have any idea who's doing it?"

Ben shrugged in frustration. "No one is saying for sure, but I think there are some kids in the town whose parents have a little too much money but not quite enough time to give them."

Frankie had been so absorbed in their conversation that she was surprised when she spotted the Nature Center again and realized they had walked in a circle.

Ben chuckled a bit ruefully as he noticed the same thing.

"Dad likes to walk," he said. "It helps calm him. If you don't mind, we could make another loop, and this time I'll show off my tour-guide skills."

Frankie sensed the effort Ben was making to be hospitable and how difficult it must be for him to find balance in his life. A tiny piece of armor fell from her heart.

"Are you okay to walk a bit more?" she asked Rae.

"Sure," Rae answered cheerily. "Al and I are having a good chat."

Frankie was happy that Rae was comfortable. It was what she wanted for her daughter. But she couldn't help wondering how any kind of attachment to their summer neighbors—even a minor one—would impact their time and her own aspirations.

Later, while Ben scrambled eggs for supper on one of the cabin's hot plates back in what had been Frankie's cabin, he reflected on the interesting turn the day had taken. Scrambled eggs were one of Al's favorites, but it wasn't really his dad that Ben thought about as he pushed the eggs around the pan and opened the fridge to locate the bread. He was grateful that the Lord had kept his father safe today, and he was surprised at the role Frankie had played.

He thought about how her direct gaze seemed to compel him to do things like give up his cabin. He wished he knew more of Frankie's story, but sensed that she would be very reluctant to share it.

Someone had hurt her and that little girl of hers, of that much he was sure. Despite Frankie's tough exterior, her pretense of not wanting to accept favors from anyone, Ben sensed a longing that hung around her like a cloak. He could identify with that. No matter how different the reasons were behind it, he was absolutely sure they both carried the burden of regret.

He had no doubt that she would do anything to protect her daughter, but from the way she had readily stepped forward to defend his dad, it seemed that her protective instincts didn't stop at Rae.

She possessed a complexity of traits and Ben realized that he found that very appealing. The kinds of women he had always dated were the ones he had grown up with at church. They had all known each other from the time they had been angels and shepherds in the Christmas pageant, through youth groups and confirmation classes, all the way to some of them getting married and having kids. He had been on good enough terms with all of them, but there hadn't been a single one he could have envisioned a future with. Maybe that was because he had always felt as if he was playing a role—the role of the pastor's son.

He was thirty and had never married. He had never met a woman who he felt he could be completely himself with. Then he had been called to do missionary work, or at least what he told himself was the call. Now, with all he was coping with and preparing for in regard to his father, it was the last thing on his mind.

Ben put Al's favorite mug on the table, the one with the picture of a fat Canada goose on it, and poured chocolate milk into it. The rather smug look on the goose's face always made him chuckle.

"What are you laughing at, son?"

Ah, there it was. Ben stopped short against the tormenting bliss of it. It was one of those rare moments of lucidity—he had heard other caregivers talk of it—when your loved one returned for a moment to being the person you had known.

He swallowed and said, "I was just looking at this." He pointed to the goose. "Supper's almost ready. Are you hungry?"

As quickly as it came, Al slipped back behind the gray gauze where no one could reach him. He stamped his foot and waved his arms at his son.

"Nope! Nope!"

Ben managed to get him to sit down and put ketchup on his scrambled eggs the way Al liked it. He bowed his head and gave thanks for their supper.

"Amen," Al said dutifully. There were some things he always remembered.

Despite his best efforts to push the thought to the back of his mind, Ben's stomach roiled at the images of the care facility that would be necessary by the end of the summer. He watched his father eat without much appetite himself.

Bits of conversation and laughter drifted in from other cabins. Ben could hear the sound of bikes going down the path and of music playing in the distance. He wondered what Frankie and Rae were having for supper. Probably something more exciting than scrambled eggs, he mused.

But he had to ask himself why he was thinking about her. Clearly she had walls as thick as cement and he had enough to deal with right now. He also suspected that her life was consumed with her own worries and concerns.

A loud squeak of dismay permeated the air. Was that Frankie? Ben half rose from his chair.

"It's okay! We've got this!" Yes, that was her voice, no doubt reassuring Rae about something. There was a clatter and an audible gasp.

Ben couldn't help himself—he had to look out the door and see what was going on.

He watched from the doorway as Frankie made a valid attempt to light the barbecue grill on their deck. The flames went from nonexistent to a fiery roar.

It would embarrass her if he went right out there, Ben reasoned. Besides, if he was being totally honest with himself, he found himself caught up in just watching her. Finding her as attractive as he did unsettled him, but he couldn't help it.

That brief moment when he had thought she was a boy had completely disappeared into the land of the absurd. In her blue jean shorts and light plaid blouse, she was indisputably feminine. No longer under the ball cap, her hair was pulled up into a ponytail that swayed and bounced and almost seemed to have a personality of its own as Frankie leaned closer to the flames and then jumped back again. It was a deep auburn color, with the sun kissing it here and there into shades of strawberry blonde.

"Maybe Ben can help us?" Ben heard Rae offer.

"Ben?" Frankie stopped her maneuverings and put her hands on her hips. "No, honey, we're not going to ask him for any more help."

She stood with her hands anchored to her hips and her legs slightly apart, and looked around as if hoping the solution would come by carried on the breeze.

When her eyes fell on Ben, she froze. Then her cheeks flushed pink.

"How long have you been there?" she asked.

# Chapter Three

"Not long," Ben said. He knew she didn't want to be seen as incompetent "I heard a noise and I wanted to make sure you were okay."

"I'm fine."

Ben looked at her, looked at the raging fire and back at her again. His mouth twitched as he tried to suppress a grin.

"I can see that," he said with mock seriousness.

"Are you laughing at me?" She still looked upset, but he could tell that she was also starting to see the humor in the situation.

"I would never do that," Ben said in an overly solemn tone, placing his hand on his heart with a dramatic gesture.

Rae giggled heartily, and they both turned to look at her.

Frankie's face was wreathed in pleased surprise. "I haven't heard that sound for a while," she admitted, and then snapped her mouth shut as if to keep herself from revealing more.

"Mom, can he please just start the fire for us?" Rae begged. "I'm totally starving and then we could probably eat in, like, ten minutes."

"Your daughter's pretty smart," Ben said. "She makes a lot of sense for—an eight-year-old?" he guessed.

"I'm ten," Rae corrected him, fixing him with a flat look that made him chuckle again. It was abundantly clear what she thought of his age-guessing abilities.

"Now what's funny?" Frankie asked.

"Nothing… It's just that her expression reminded me very much of you."

"How can you say that when you don't even know me," Frankie retorted.

Oh, but somehow he felt like he did, Ben thought. And he didn't want to because he didn't need his life to get more complicated.

He clapped his hands together, briskly, and said, "How about it? I could show you how to manage this temperamental beast now, and next time it's all you."

"Well, I guess so," Frankie agreed reluctantly. "But then you and your dad must join us for supper because you've already done enough for us. That is, if you haven't already eaten."

"We just started eating," Ben said. He did a quick check over his shoulder at Al, who was flattening his eggs with his fork, but still in his chair.

"Well…" Frankie hesitated.

*"Mom!"* demanded Rae.

"Listen to your daughter," Ben urged.

A few minutes later, he had the flames licking and spitting at a reasonable rate, having been careful to explain to Frankie what he had done.

Ben felt inordinately pleased when Frankie quickly mastered the fire as he had shown her, and cautioned himself not to get too involved.

Within a few weeks at Silver Lake, Frankie and Rae had fallen into a comfortable rhythm, the kind that Frankie had almost forgotten could exist since everything at home reminded her of what they had lost. Here, in this new setting, she found that looking ahead, rather than back, was starting to feel more natural.

Early in the morning, Frankie took her coffee out onto the deck while Rae was still sleeping and enjoyed the way the day quietly unfolded before more people began to stir. She loved the smell of the pine from the trees and the fresh wind off the lake. Occasionally, a smattering of other early risers passed by, with morning newspapers under their arms, as they headed down to get coffee and sit at the tables in front of the Beachfront Confectionery and bakeshop. They waved and smiled in greeting, and Frankie waved and smiled back.

Previously, the early mornings and the peaceful setting would have been an opportune time to do a morning devotional, but she knew it would take more time for her to make progress in that area.

She was grateful that, slowly but surely, her daughter was taking steps out of the cave she had created for herself. She loved the beach and the Nature Center and going for ice cream. Rae had started to make observations again, with her artist's eye, commenting on colors and the proximity of shapes and textures—solid rocks at the edge of the ever-changing water; mossy grass swallowing up the bark-rough base of a tree—and Frankie dared to hope that a full-fledged return to her art was imminent.

But Rae was also, in Frankie's opinion, just a little too fond of wanting to know what Ben and Al were doing. It was a frequent reminder to Frankie that she wasn't nearly as oblivious to her summer neighbor as she wanted to be—as she *needed* to be.

She'd have to be blind not to notice how good-looking Ben was with those dark blue eyes that provided such great contrast to the wheat and sunshine of his hair. But she wasn't going to think about that.

She also wasn't going to think about his rugged chin or the funny expression he got when he was trying not to laugh.

The screen door of the cabin banged and startled her.

"What time is it?" Rae asked, poking her head out of the door.

"It's early, Sweet Pea, really early. What are you doing up?"

Frankie looked affectionately at her daughter, wearing her SpongeBob pajamas, her hair a fuzzy cloud around her face.

"I'm excited for today."

"Today?" Frankie teased, "Hmm, what's today?"

"Mom!"

Frankie winked at her and reached out an arm to pull her in for a little side hug.

"I know. But you'll have to be excited for a little while longer. The Nature Center doesn't even open for a couple more hours. You'll have to find something to keep you busy until then."

The day before, when they had visited the Nature Center, there was a sign advertising that anyone interested could go there to learn about how the displays were put together and then how to make displays of their own.

It had warmed Frankie's heart to see Rae's enthusiasm. Maybe it was true, she mused, that there was something healing about the lake. Did she dare to hope that it could do the same for her? If she could be satisfied that Rae was back to her ardent, artistic self, would Frankie then feel free to unearth the dreams in her own heart?

Rae bounced up and down a little. "Can I have something for breakfast?"

"If you're hungry, you know where the cereal and milk are, or there's toast."

Her daughter wrinkled her snub nose. "That's boring."

"Well, it's what we've got." Frankie gave her one more squeeze and stood up to stretch and take her coffee cup in for a refill.

"What time do you think Ben and Al will get up?" Rae looked in the direction of their cabin.

The cleaning crews had done their best and the side of the cabin looked much better than it had, but a gray dinginess still lurked as a reminder under the fresh paint. There also continued to be graffiti that showed up randomly on other cabins and buildings. No one knew who the culprit or culprits were, or if they did, they weren't saying. Frankie wondered if Ben was right about the rich parents and their children who had too much time to get into trouble. She didn't like the way it hummed like an out-of-tune buzzing underneath the harmony of the summer days.

"Mom!" Rae tugged her hand, letting her know she hadn't been listening.

Oh yes, Ben and Al…again.

Frankie was going to try this one more time. "Look, Sweet Pea, I think that Ben and his dad probably want some quiet time to enjoy the summer. Remember that Al is sick."

"He doesn't look sick."

"Well, it isn't the kind of sick that you can always see." Frankie tried to think of a way to explain. "I told you that Al has Alzheimer's disease."

Rae shifted from one foot to the other. "Is that when people forget stuff?"

"Well, that's mostly what people think of when they hear about Alzheimer's, and that does happen. It's kind of like when you have all the pieces of a puzzle and you just can't think of how to make them fit together. Al might recognize a lot of the things around him but when he tries to put it into a whole picture it doesn't make sense to him, and that's why he gets upset sometimes."

"Because he's scared?" Rae asked very softly.

"Yes, Sweet Pea, that's exactly right."

After a few seconds of silence Rae asked, "Will Nana and Pops get it?"

Frankie thought of her parents. They were probably up early, too, and working in their garden. They were both healthy, but one never knew for sure. Ben had said he'd thought his father would be the last person to suffer from it.

"I don't think that's something we need to worry about today," she said. "Now, why don't you go get your breakfast and pick out the clothes you're going to wear."

Frankie followed Rae inside and decided to forgo another cup of coffee and have a glass of water instead. After she made sure that Rae had what she needed, she went back onto the deck, taking the morning newspaper with the hope of absorbing herself in the crossword puzzle.

Outside she saw Ben across the way on their deck and she considered dashing back inside again before he spotted her. But it was too late. He lifted his coffee mug in a kind of salute. Then he pointed at himself and at her, with his eyebrows raised in a question, asking if he could join her.

Frankie groaned under her breath. Naturally, she thought wryly, first thing in the morning and he had to look like a male model advertising the virtues of the great outdoors. She didn't even want to think of what she must look like to him with her bedhead hair and her grubby lounge wear. She wished she could say no and go back inside, but she couldn't think of a way to do it now without it being rude.

Ben had purposely got up early to get some quiet time in before his day was taken over by his father's constant needs. When he spotted Frankie on her own deck, he guessed that she, too, must need the quiet. He could only imagine that single-mom duties could easily overtake her day, as well. But the next thing he knew, he was asking to join her, almost as if he had no will of his own. Or was he just using her as a pleasant distraction from the regrets that almost constantly haunted him?

"Ah, the morning crossword puzzle," Ben said. He spotted the pencil in her hand. "Not brave enough to do it in ink?" he teased her.

She fixed him with what he'd already begun to think of as "the Frankie face" and said, deadpan, "I don't want to show off."

Ben made himself at home in the other chair and took a sip of his coffee.

"Is Rae still asleep?"

"No, she's inside having breakfast and getting ready. I wish she had slept in a bit later," Frankie confessed. "I signed her up for those classes at the Nature Center and she's pretty excited about it."

Ben nodded his acknowledgment. From Frankie's expression, it was evident that she was happy Rae had something to look forward to.

"Dad used to love crossword puzzles," he mused. "He was really good at them, too."

"You said he was a minister?" Frankie asked. "Have you followed in his footsteps?"

"No." Ben shook his head. Many things rushed through his mind that he could offer as a way of explanation, but he decided to stick with the basic facts. "I'm a general contractor, but I did want to do something worthwhile, so I've been on a few mission trips to help with construction and repairs. I also did a bit of work with literacy programs. It was great sharing Jesus with people in a way that felt natural to me."

Frankie didn't say anything, and after a moment she looked down at her crossword puzzle. "What's a five-letter word for *angry*?"

The deliberate change in conversation didn't slip by Ben. Tread carefully, he reminded himself, for his own sake as well as hers. He was curious about her faith and sensed that it was a struggle for her, but he had his own struggles. A Christian upbringing didn't mean faith was always easy. Sometimes, he thought, it actually made it more difficult.

Ben returned his thoughts to the question. "What does it start with?" he asked.

"I"

"Irate?"

Frankie considered it. "Yes, that works." She wrote the word in carefully.

"So, Rae likes the Nature Center," Ben said. "How do you plan to keep yourself busy for the next couple of months?"

It was hard, he mused, to make casual conversation when the thought of how appealing she looked floated up like a ginger ale bubble in him.

She tucked her hair behind her ears. In the morning light, the color looked like a sunrise.

"I like to walk and look at things," Frankie told him. "I enjoy sitting down by the water to watch the waves and think."

He had the distinct impression that she had much more planned than that, but her expression was closed, not allowing further questions.

"My mom was a schoolteacher," he shared, sensing it would be better to talk about other things. "What about your parents? Are they both…?"

"Alive, yes," she said. "And, thankfully, they're

healthy, too. We all live in Regina. It's about a six-hour drive from here."

"We're from Saskatoon," Ben said. "Is this your first time here at the lake?"

Frankie nodded. "I'd heard good things about it. I figured it sounded like a perfect place for us to…" Ben could almost see her swallowing a word. "For us to have fun," she finished.

Ben gave a rueful chuckle. "I guess I'm hoping that something here will still be meaningful to Dad. I'm quite certain this will be our last trip here together." It surprised him that he had said the words out loud, but somehow having them fall on other ears took away a trace of the sting in his throat.

They sat in silence for a moment. Frankie put down her pencil. Through the window screen, they could hear Rae humming to herself.

"She likes it here," Frankie said with a smile that softened her face.

"You're a good mom," Ben said. He felt those words were inadequate, but it was the best he could come up with.

"Thank you. I try."

Frankie studied her hands, then set her gaze directly on him.

"I do my best. It hasn't been easy for us on our own." She lifted her chin and her expression told Ben that she wasn't providing any more details—not now and maybe not ever.

He wanted to let her know in some way that he understood. Oh, he definitely understood what it meant to step into a void you weren't at all confident you could fill.

"I feel that way about Dad sometimes," he admitted. "I don't know how many times a day I just wish I had someone to compare notes with. I mean, there are support groups and all but…"

Frankie nodded in agreement.

"Will your dad be okay with you over here?"

"He was sound asleep when I left, but I should go check on him soon. Frankie?"

"Yes?"

"I was wondering if it would be okay if we walked to the Nature Center with you and Rae. Dad's usually better about eating his breakfast if he gets a walk first."

He could see her hesitate slightly. Then she spoke.

"That's fine. I'm sure Rae would like that."

*I like this blouse*, Frankie told herself as she got dressed. She'd wear it anyway. It had nothing to do with the fact that she always got compliments about how well the color suited her. It had nothing to do with her wanting Ben to know she could look much better than she had this morning.

Rae had been ready to go for half an hour at least and was bouncing around, making her braids swing. Her glasses slid down her nose and she pushed them back up.

"Can I go outside and see if Ben and Al are ready to go?" she asked. As Frankie had anticipated, she was happy to have them along.

"You're like a jumping bean," Frankie teased. "Go ahead. I'll be out soon."

She glanced at her reflection in the small mirror on one of the walls, fluffed her hair a bit, added some lip gloss and decided she looked okay.

When Ben greeted her, she thought she saw a light of admiration in his eyes. Yet, her stomach sifted in confusion. She couldn't explain to herself why she wanted him to admire her.

"C'mon! C'mon!" Al demanded.

"Let's go!" Rae agreed.

Frankie caught Ben's look and they shared a quiet smile over the similar restlessness of his aging father and her young daughter.

As they walked to the Nature Center, Frankie breathed the fresh pine-filled air, and enjoyed the sights and sounds of people ready to make the most of the day.

*I feel happy.* The thought entered her mind

cautiously, not sure of its welcome. It was more than just being a mother who was happy because her daughter was: it was the beginning of her own personal happiness that came with finally starting to believe that the worst was over.

"Mom, what's that?" Rae pointed as they neared the Nature Center.

Frankie looked and the thought of being happy skittered away.

"What in the world…?" Ben quickened his pace.

A group of people stood by the entrance of the center and milled about, talking loudly and asking one another questions that could not be answered.

The door was barred shut and the building had been brutalized with wild streaks of red and black. Most chilling of all was the proclamation painted across the side—I HATE EVERYBODY!

Frankie felt Ben grab her hand. She looked quickly at his face and saw that it had been an unthinking gesture.

"It's getting worse," he said.

## *Chapter Four*

Ben hadn't meant to grab Frankie's hand, but when he saw her face turn white with shock, he wondered if he'd have to put his arms around her to keep her steady on her feet.

Then she stabilized and immediately concerned herself with Rae.

"I'm so sorry, Sweet Pea," she said to her daughter, whose eyes were welling up with the cruel disappointment of the situation.

Frankie excavated her hand from Ben's and gathered Rae into a hug.

"Shh," she said gently, patting Rae's back. "I know you're disappointed, but we'll find something else to do." Above Rae's head, Frankie's face was stricken and Ben could see her willing herself to stay strong for her daughter.

Ben fought a surge of anger and frustration. No one needed this vandalism to ruin and complicate their summers. Why was God allowing this to happen when he'd had such a simple hope—just to have a chance to feel right with his father again? And it was clear that Frankie needed something from the summer for her and Rae, too. Even if it was just to relax and have fun, why couldn't they have that? Was it too much to ask?

He wondered how he could best offer comfort to them, and then Al shifted restlessly beside him and made a rumbling, whining noise in his throat.

"That—that—girl." He pointed at Rae.

"Yes, she's sad." *We're all sad*, he wanted to add, and maybe the saddest thing of all was that there was a time that he would have understood—a time when he would have been the first to offer comfort—but now he didn't understand at all.

Ben looked around, assessing the situation. He wanted to ask for details, to see if anyone there had seen or heard anything suspicious before this latest incident. He patted the pockets of his shorts, hoping he would find something he could give to his dad to keep him preoccupied. He spotted three stones on the ground of similar size and shape. He helped Al to get crouched down and demonstrated how to put the stones in rows.

"Have you heard anything, Brent?" he asked one of the men standing nearby whom he'd known for several years.

"Not much. But some kids were walking home after the late show and they say it was fine when they passed it. That would have been around eleven thirty last night."

"Is there damage to the inside? Is that why the doors are barred?" His building contractor's mind automatically began to speculate and make assessments.

Brent shrugged helplessly. "Can't say for sure. Probably, and if there is, well, we all know that means this has gone from inconvenient to something much worse. All I know right now is that there are a lot of very disappointed kids."

"I know," Ben said grimly. Was this his time to step up and fill the void that his dad would have filled? Was he meant to offer a solution or at least some comfort and reassurance?

*Please guide me, Lord.*

A quick glance told Ben that his father was still occupied with the stones. His gaze then sought out Frankie and Rae and he saw that they were engaged in conversation with the volunteer who'd had the run-in with Al.

Anxiety nudged at him, as he thought of the unfortunate incident involving his father. He wanted to make sure the volunteer wasn't going to harass Frankie. At the same time, though, he wasn't sure how long he could trust the reprieve from his father's demands.

Al scooped up the stones, looked at them a moment and then began to line them up again, carefully, one by one. Ben took the opportunity to make his way quickly to Frankie.

"Is everything okay here?" he asked, keeping his tone light as he searched Frankie's face for any signs of additional stress.

But when she turned to acknowledge him, her face was soft, her eyes bright.

"Yes," she said. "I'm just having a nice chat with Lydia here."

Lydia nodded at Ben and had the good grace to look chagrined.

"I recognized Frankie from the other day," she confessed. "I wanted to find you and apologize. I feel horrible about the way I acted."

"Apology accepted," Ben said. "I usually keep close tabs on him, but he slipped away from me that morning, so I apologize for what happened, too. I know Dad's outbursts can be frightening but he can't help it."

"I realize that now," Lydia said. "Frankie here was helping me understand a few things about the disease. You're lucky to have a friend who cares so much about you and your dad."

Ben's eyes sought Frankie's and he was surprised when she blushed, but couldn't help feeling a bit pleased about it. He told himself that was only because it was nice for anyone to discover they had support.

"I know," he said softly. "We are very lucky."

"Well, again, I am sorry," Lydia said. "It's no excuse, but things really have been stressful around here. Everyone is on edge, not knowing who to trust, wondering who's going to get hit next." She shook her head ruefully. "I guess we got our answer this morning."

Frankie put her hands on Rae's shoulders. Rae, Ben thought, looked like a sad and deflated balloon compared to her buoyancy of just a few minutes ago.

"Isn't there somewhere else they could teach a class," he asked, "even if it's just art and they're not able to build the displays?" He thought for a moment and snapped his fingers as realization struck him.

"What about over at the library? They have extra rooms over there. One of them should work for an art class."

"I'll go ask," Lydia said. With a decisive nod she headed off.

"Don't worry, we'll get this fixed," Ben told Rae.

Above her daughter's head, Frankie's face showed her disconcertment.

"We?" she asked.

"I just thought…"

"Please don't."

"Don't what?" Ben couldn't help the humor that quirked his mouth. "Think?"

She rewarded him with a roll of her expressive brown eyes.

"Please don't think that you have to fix everything for us."

"I didn't think it would hurt to ask if other arrangements could be made." He scanned the group and located his father. "I have to get back to Dad. I hope Rae gets to do her art today. I know how much she was looking forward to it."

"We'll figure it out," Frankie said.

An uneasy silence hung between them. Frankie angled her body slightly in the other direction and gave Rae's shoulders a little squeeze.

A few seconds later, Lydia came bustling back to them, looking slightly out of breath.

"There's a room at the library," she announced. "The kids can do art there, and they can stay and see what other activities are going on or just look at books, whatever they want. If your little girl would like to come, you can walk her over in about half an hour—they just need some time to get set up—and you can pick her up at lunchtime, if that's okay."

"What do you think?" Frankie asked Rae. "Would you like to go?"

Rae shrugged, then looked up and nodded. A soft light began to make its way back into her eyes.

Ben was relieved he was there to see it. Whether Frankie wanted his help or not, he didn't know if he could just sit back and do nothing when he could help in some way—not only them but the whole town. So far the vandalism had just been sprayed paint and graffiti, but if there was now the possibility of fixing and rebuilding to be done, he had expertise to contribute in that area and wanted to do so.

He knew he couldn't make up for the times he had been absent—they were over and gone—but at least he could do this. His heart clenched as the thought came that he wished his dad could be proud of him. Then he felt that familiar rip of divided emotions when he recalled that his caregiver's role was growing by the day. He didn't know how he would find the time to manage his father and do something for the community, as well.

"Thank you," Frankie said to Lydia. It seemed she had chosen to ignore Ben's role in the backup plan.

Ben walked back to Al, who gave up his stones without a fuss and allowed Ben to lead him by the hand back to where Frankie and Lydia were chatting.

Frankie asked Lydia, "How's this all going to get cleaned up? Is there anything we can do to help?"

"I'll let you know," Lydia said. "I'm sure there'll be a meeting of some kind to figure out a plan." She grimaced slightly. "I should say, yet *another* plan. Anyway, thanks for asking."

"Keep me posted, too," Ben interjected. "You're new here, Lydia, so you don't know that I have a general contracting company and I'd be happy to offer my advice and assistance any way I can."

"Thank you, we appreciate that," Lydia said. "Speaking of helping out, I'd better get back up there and see what I can do."

"What are you going to do while Rae's at her art class?" Ben asked. He tried to pass it off as a simple conversational question, but he was genuinely curious.

Frankie shrugged her shoulders and looked slightly wary. "I don't have any real plans. Maybe go for a walk or something." Once again, Ben had the distinct impression that she had plans she didn't wish to share with him. There was really no reason she should, he reminded himself.

"Dad will want to walk, too, if you don't mind…?" He let the question hang between them.

"Maybe I'll catch up with you later," Frankie answered, after a pause. "After I take Rae to the library." Her face was unreadable and she didn't quite meet his eyes.

"I'll be back here right at noon to get you," Frankie told Rae as she got her settled at the library. "So, don't worry and…"

"I'm not worried, Mom," Rae said. "Don't *you* worry—go have fun."

Frankie smiled at her daughter's rather parental proclamation and kissed Rae on the top of her head.

"I'll do my best."

Sometimes when she was separated from Rae, Frankie felt slightly at a loss over what she would do to pass the time. It was a familiar sensation to the one she had at home when Rae was out playing with a friend—in the days before she had become so withdrawn—or having a sleepover at Nana and Pops's house.

She considered remaining at the library, telling herself that it would be relaxing to find a magazine to read. It didn't take long to dismiss that idea. No doubt, Rae would find it *lame*, as she described things that did not impress her, to have her mother hovering while she was in class. Besides, Frankie reminded herself, she was here to consider how to get her own life back in order, too, and to simply enjoy the beautiful surroundings.

Frankie wondered what Ben was doing and then rapidly tried to stop. But a disturbing truth nudged at her heart. She was upset with herself in the ways she had let him into their lives already and wanted to put a halt to that before she found herself unwittingly dependent on him. Because he was bound to let her down—that's what men did.

She decided to go for a walk and take the time to check out some of the shops, which she had not done thoroughly yet. She thought she might also pop back around to the Nature Center to see if Lydia had found anything else out about the help that was needed.

Things had certainly taken an interesting turn with regard to Lydia. After the way they had met, Frankie hadn't expected an apology or the sense that she and the volunteer worker might actually get along. The women in a small Bible study group that Frankie had once belonged to would call it a "God thing," an idea that she immediately wanted to dismiss…yet, it lingered faintly with her.

Lydia, Frankie thought, might be a refreshing change: she was a little rough around the edges, but she had readily admitted her wrong-doing and Frankie thought there was a lot of promise in that.

A stop by the Nature Center revealed that it was still locked up, and the crowd had dispersed except for a police officer and a man discussing something. Frankie couldn't hear their words, but the tension in their body postures made it apparent that it wasn't an easy conversation. The suit the man wore was a loud declaration that he was a visitor and not part of the regular beach community.

The problem, Frankie thought, as she looked around for Lydia, was that her time hadn't really felt like her own for years, and now that she had it she hardly knew what to do with herself.

She couldn't see Lydia anywhere, so she kept walking.

Frankie recalled the way her ex-husband had frequently reminded her that she was lucky to have him, always pointing out what he considered flaws in her appearance and shortcomings in her personality.

Ben wouldn't treat his wife that way. The thought came unbidden and rattled her.

She heard footsteps hurrying up behind her and turned to see Lydia catching up.

"Did you come by the center again?" Lydia

asked. "Sorry if I missed you. My boss wanted to look around inside and see if there's damage in there but the police don't want us to move or touch anything, so they've sent me on an early break while they decide what needs to be done next."

"I'm a bit at loose ends myself," Frankie confessed. "I'm just walking, if you want to join me."

Lydia fell into place beside her.

"What else is being said?" Frankie asked. "About the vandalism, I mean?"

"Not too much, at least to me," Lydia said. "As you can probably tell, I'm a bit of a fish out of water here—no pun intended. I was supposed to be helping the curator at the Western Development Museum in Saskatoon, but that fell through at the last minute, so I ended up here. It's not bad, just not what I'd hoped for."

Frankie thought about how familiar she was with the feeling of things not working out the way she hoped.

"Hey, he's pretty good-looking. Ben, I mean," Lydia said. "How long have you been friends?"

"A little while," Frankie murmured vaguely. For a moment, she was tempted to divulge her ruse, but Lydia started talking about something else and the moment passed.

"You seem like a bit of a fish out of water,

too," Lydia said bluntly. "I mean, I can tell you don't know people around here the way your friend does. So, what's your story?"

Frankie had been so used to avoiding the topic and feeling constantly burdened with shame that she was surprised to hear the words "I'm divorced," come out of her mouth. And even more surprised to feel how good it felt to say them to someone she didn't have any history with or owe any explanation to.

Lydia just nodded. "That's tough," she said. "So—what's next?"

"That's what I'm trying to figure out this summer."

"You'll get there," Lydia said in a comfortable way. "Do you journal? I find that's a good way to sort through things and figure out where you want life to take you. It always works for me."

The thought came into Frankie's mind that Lydia didn't look like the journaling type, but she was learning that you could never tell what people had inside of them—good or bad—by how they looked.

"That might be a good idea," she said, pondering. "Is there somewhere in town that sells journals?"

"Maeve's Miscellaneous. It's right beside the beauty salon. We can walk that way, if you like."

Frankie nodded. "I know where that is."

Maeve's Miscellaneous was an overcrowded shop that, true to its name, featured an eclectic collection of items ranging from kitchen gadgets and packets of spices to silk scarves and handcrafted jewelry.

"The journals are usually up by the front," Lydia said, leading Frankie through the maze. "Ah, yes, here we are."

Frankie selected one that had a white cover with a monarch butterfly on the front—it reminded her that she, too, was on a long journey of sorts.

"So, what do you think you'll write about?" Lydia asked when they were back outside again. "Your goals? Never mind—you don't have to tell me if you don't want to."

"I want to become a nurse," Frankie said. Once again, it felt good to say the words out loud. She explained the work she had done up to this point and how she felt she had an affinity for it and could do more if she was properly trained.

"Write it down," Lydia urged. "If you write it down, you'll have a better chance of really committing to it." She looked at her watch. "I have to get back to the center. Listen, you should take one of the delicious cinnamon buns from the Beachfront Confectionery, go down to the beach, and take your journal there and just write. Maybe write your questions about him, too."

"Him?" Frankie asked.

"Your friend, Ben. And don't even pretend that you haven't wondered if you could ever be more than friends. The air is pretty thick between you two."

Her head buzzing with Lydia's comment about Ben, Frankie bought a cinnamon bun at the Beachfront Confectionery and carried it and her journal to a relatively quiet spot on the beach. She positioned herself half in the shade, rested back against a rather large rock, opened her journal and paused. She looked out at the water and took a reflective bite of the bun.

It took some effort, but she pushed Lydia's parting remarks to the back of her mind. She meant well, Frankie was sure, but clearly she didn't always know what she was talking about. She took the last bite, and dusted the cinnamon and sugar off her fingers with a napkin. She opened her journal and quickly, decisively, wrote, "Become a Nurse" and circled it three times.

Immediately, dissenting thoughts began to quarrel with her: *Where will you get the money? What about Rae? Shouldn't her needs come first? You've been out of school for a lot of years now, Frankie. Are you sure you're not just setting yourself up to fail?*

She put her pen to the side and clenched the new journal, willing herself not to succumb to the negative thoughts. She looked out at the water and tried to use its gently rolling pulse as a way to focus and calm herself.

Then she heard, faintly, a shout in the distance.

She turned her head in the direction of the noise and could see Ben and Al standing on a dock, at the end closest to the water.

It was funny, Frankie mused with a strange twinge in her stomach. She knew with complete certainty it was them, even from her vantage point. She would like to be able to say that it was only Al's hunched, apprehensive posture, typical of those with Alzheimer's, that gave them away. But the truth was that her eyes would know the strong lines of Ben's physique anywhere. Lydia's observation pushed its way back to the forefront of her thoughts again.

She couldn't help watching them to see what they were doing.

It appeared that Ben was trying to draw his father's attention to something. He had his hand on one of Al's shoulders and seemed to be trying to gently turn him while he pointed out at the water.

Al kept moving his shoulder out from Ben's touch. Frankie could see by his body language that he was becoming increasingly agitated. His voice grew louder as he began to shift quickly, almost frantically back and forth.

She could see Ben trying to soothe him, trying to take hold of his father's arms, which Al had begun to thrash around.

Then Al suddenly stopped and, in a quicksilver flash, his arms shot out, his hands pushing hard at Ben's chest.

Frankie gasped as she watched Ben stumble back, frantically spinning his arms to regain his balance. His efforts failed and he flew off the dock, landing in the water with a large splash.

# Chapter Five

One of Ben's first coherent thoughts was that he couldn't believe he had forgotten just how cold a northern Saskatchewan lake could be. The icy shock of the water snatched away his breath and his reasoning, so it took a few panicked seconds for him to realize that the water wasn't deep and that he could simply stand up.

His second coherent thought was for his father, and he got out of the water as quickly as he could, calling out for his dad.

Al had left the dock but, thankfully, he hadn't gone far. His outburst had subsided as suddenly as it had come on and he looked at Ben, his tongue poking out of the corner of his mouth.

"Baptized," he said.

"Very funny, Dad," Ben mumbled, but it was one of those moments that both encouraged and confused him. On the one hand, his dad never would have done something like this if the disease wasn't advancing; on the other hand, if he could still make the connection between water and baptism…? How was Ben supposed to know the right decision in the matter of putting his father in a home?

He heard the soft, smacking sound of bare feet on sand and turned to see Frankie as she hurried toward them.

"Are you okay?" she gasped out as she neared them.

Ben registered almost automatically how attractive she looked with her cheeks slightly flushed from her jog over and her sunrise hair tumbling around her delicate face. But what really caught his attention was the look of concern in her eyes. Was it possible that she wasn't as guarded and aloof as she made herself out to be?

"I'm fine," Ben assured her. "I was just caught off guard and that water is cold, with a capital *C*!"

"What happened out there?" she asked.

"I'm not totally sure. I was trying to show Dad the water. When I was a boy we used to walk out on that dock all the time, and we'd sit and look out at the water and talk about God and life—whatever was on our minds."

Ben paused as appreciation and regret tussled for his attention.

"Anyway, I thought he might still like to look at the water, even if we couldn't visit the way we used to. Clearly, I was wrong."

"He's probably afraid of the water," Frankie suggested gently. "I don't know why it happens, but many who have Alzheimer's are." She chuckled rather dolefully. "I can tell you that bath time at the home where I work isn't always a lot of fun."

"I can imagine."

Suddenly conscious of the water streaming off him and pooling around his feet, Ben tore his eyes away from Frankie's face.

"I guess I'd better get back up to the cabin and change," he said. "Good thing it's such a warm day."

She gave one of her snorts, which caused Ben to grin. He still wasn't used to the incongruity of that sound coming from her rosebud mouth. A moment later, when he looked at her face again, she was pensive.

"Are *you* okay?" Ben asked.

She shrugged and tried to smile, but it didn't quite reach her eyes.

"Yes. I've just got a lot on my mind."

"On holidays?" he prodded gently.

Frankie chewed her lip and looked like she was pondering how much she should tell him. Then a grunt from Al signaled that he had run out of patience. Besides, Ben's clothes were still dripping.

"Do you want to walk back up with us?" Ben asked. Briefly he wondered if he should ask for her input on how she thought his dad was doing, but he dismissed that idea quickly. Clearly, they both had their own issues to work through.

Frankie shook her head. "No, thanks. I came over here so fast to see if you were okay that I left some things where I was sitting. I'll have to go get them and I'll probably check on Rae soon."

Ben nodded. "I hope she had a fun morning—I mean, after the way it started."

"I hope so, too," Frankie said. "I walked by the center again, but there wasn't much going on. I saw Lydia."

"I hope you watch your step around her," Ben grumbled. He was still struggling to get past his first impression but felt bad for that at the same time. Wasn't he supposed to be a person who had learned how to forgive, especially since he was a person who needed forgiveness?

"She's an okay person," Frankie said. "I promise." She reached out and gave his arm a gentle, reassuring squeeze. Then she dropped her hand suddenly, as if something had electrocuted her, mumbled something about the time and hurried away.

The warmth of her touch seemed to penetrate through the dampness of Ben's skin and set off an explosion of questions in his mind.

As he walked along with his father back up to their cabin, keeping an eye out to make sure that Al didn't wander off or become confrontational with anyone, Ben experienced an acute pang of sadness and longing. He missed being able to talk to his dad about whatever was on his mind.

Experimentally he said, "So, Dad, what's your theory on what's been going around here? Who do you think might be doing it?"

Silence.

"What do you think of Frankie, Dad? Did you see the way she came rushing down to the dock to see if I was okay?" *Did you see the way she touched my arm?* he added silently.

But Al just looked at him and worked his face into a fret.

"Okay, Dad," Ben said. "It's okay. We're going back to the cabin."

Then he asked one last, silent question: *Have you forgiven me for not being here for you and Mom when you needed me?*

But it was too late for his dad to answer, and

not knowing for sure felt worse than anything else that was going on.

Frankie's journal and pen were right where she had left them. She still had time to add to her list, if only her mind would cooperate.

It was something she would have done with anyone, she told herself. Countless times she had touched Rae in a reassuring manner or offered comfort to the residents where she worked. It didn't mean anything more than that.

So, why did her hand continue to tingle and pulse as if it had a life of its own?

With a sigh, Frankie acknowledged that the right mood for goal setting had passed. Still, the one goal she had written down flashed at her just before she snapped the journal shut.

Firmly she pushed the remaining arguments aside. If there was any good thing to be found about her being left, it was that she had discovered her own strengths and that she could accomplish whatever she needed to. If she really wanted to be a nurse, she would make it happen.

In finding the inner strength to come to that realization, she felt she'd taken a significant step forward. She thought about the way she'd hurtled down to the docks when she had seen Ben get pushed into the water. Did her caregiving instincts fully explain that, as well as the intense urge she'd had to touch his arm? Frankie cautioned herself to keep her focus where it needed to be.

She'd never been a do-nothing kind of person. That's what the problem was. If all she did was loll around on the beach or do crossword puzzles or read on the deck, no wonder her mind was open to whatever thoughts wanted to make themselves at home there.

Crossword puzzles… That made her think of the light that danced in Ben's eyes when he teased her about not using a pen.

Frankie lifted her chin and set her shoulders. Enough was enough. Holiday or not, she was going to do something productive with the remaining couple of months they had here, and she could start by exploring the resources at the library while she waited for Rae's art class to finish.

As she walked to the library, Frankie noted that the number of people out and about was sparse, no doubt because of the upsetting incident of the morning. Frankie's heart pinched. With its assortment of shops, variety of places to eat, the beach and water, tennis courts, and other places for vacationers to spend their time, Silver Lake was designed to be the perfect place for a relaxed, carefree holiday. But someone was ruining that for everyone.

Well, she wasn't going to let that happen! She wouldn't let anyone ruin this summer and what it meant for Rae and her.

At the library, Frankie found helpful resource material online and felt encouraged when she discovered that she could take some of her prerequisites by correspondence, which meant she could fit the classes into her and Rae's schedules.

"Is there any way I could print some information?" she asked the librarian. "Or bother you for a piece of paper and a pen to jot a few things down?"

"Of course," the woman said. Frankie saw that her name tag read Heather.

Heather nodded and came around to the front of the counter to show Frankie how to print from the computer. She appeared to be in her fifties, and with her trimly cut graying hair and glasses looked like the typical image people often had of a librarian—that is until Frankie noticed the small jeweled stud in her nose and that her ears were double pierced.

Here was a woman who looked like she wasn't afraid to be her own person, and that gave Frankie a boost.

"I noticed you dropping your daughter off earlier," Heather said. "She looks like a sweet girl. I'm Heather, like my tag says. I don't think

I've seen you around. How are you enjoying our little community so far?"

"I'm Frankie," she introduced herself. "It's lovely here, although, of course, I wish…"

"The vandalism," Heather said. "Yes, don't we all?"

She sat down at a computer and plugged a password into it, then stood up. "It's all yours," she told Frankie. "Let me know if you need me for anything."

"I will. Thanks so much."

"Are you on a working holiday, then?" Heather asked.

"Not really," Frankie replied. "Well—in a manner of speaking. I have some things to figure out that I haven't made the time to do yet."

The librarian nodded sagely. "It's important to make time to figure things out. I'll leave you to it."

Frankie got absorbed in exploring the nursing courses that were offered by correspondence, which she thought would be the most viable option for her, and before she knew it, she looked up and saw Rae beelining for her, with a small smudge of crimson paint on her chin and a look of bliss that caused Frankie's heart to expand.

"Hi, Mom!"

"Hi, Sweet Pea. Looks like you had fun."

"I did! I can't wait for tomorrow!" Rae fell

into her arms and Frankie hugged her, inhaling her scent of paint and suntan lotion.

"I'm so glad to hear that. Can I see what you made?"

"It's not ready yet, Mom," Rae explained with slight exasperation. "It takes time to do these things properly. How did you spend your time, Mom? Did you enjoy yourself?"

"I did." Frankie tucked in a smile at her daughter's mature-sounding question. "Thanks for asking."

She relayed to Rae the story of Ben's impromptu dip in the lake, playing up the humor and, of course, did not mention her conflicted feelings about her own reaction to the situation.

Rae giggled. "Can we maybe go to the beach after we eat?"

"Oh, I'm pretty sure we can do that."

"Yay!" Rae gave a happy little hop, which caused a strand of hair to slip out of one of her braids. Frankie tucked it back behind Rae's ear and, in that moment, she was more content than she had been in a long time.

Back at the cabin, they ate a simple lunch of peanut-butter-and-banana sandwiches, along with carrot sticks, a glass of milk for Rae and a cup of coffee for Frankie. The restaurants in town were trendy and likely served great food, but they were also expensive, and Frankie was keeping a diligent tally of the money she spent.

Rae was in the small bedroom she'd claimed as hers changing into her bathing suit when Frankie heard a tap on the door.

"Hey, it's me," Ben called through the door. "You busy?"

"Um, just getting ready to go to the beach with Rae," Frankie responded, watching her hands automatically smooth her shorts and then reach up to her hair.

"Okay, I won't keep you long, but do you have a minute?"

"Is it your father? Is he okay?" Frankie flung open the door. She forced herself to ignore that he looked decidedly enticing with a fresh shirt and his tousled hair.

"What?" Ben looked slightly startled at her sudden appearance. "No. I mean, no, it's not about Dad. He's okay—he's having a nap."

"What, then?" Frankie asked.

Seeing Ben brought her rush of confused emotions back. She attempted to mask them by a brusque tone, folded arms and a tapping foot.

"I just wanted to thank you for earlier. I mean for coming over to see if I was okay."

Frankie shifted and looked at her feet, trying to compose her face.

"Anyone would have done the same, I'm

sure," she said, looking up again and willing herself to meet his eyes firmly. "And," she added for good measure, "I would have done the same for anyone."

"I'm sure you would have," Ben said, and she couldn't quite interpret his tone. Frankie refused to cave in under the intensity of his blue-eyed scrutiny.

"I came here to talk to you about something else, too."

Frankie kept a nonchalant exterior, despite the questions that swirled through her.

"I just wanted to let you know that they'll probably be calling another community meeting soon for anyone who wants to help with cleanup and painting and such. There's no pressure, but you mentioned that you'd like to help in some way, so I wanted to let you know you'd be welcome to come if you're interested."

"I was…" Frankie hesitated. "I mean, I am interested." She considered her renewed determination to meet her own goals. But, more than that, she had to admit she was uneasy about purposely choosing an activity that could mean spending more time with Ben.

"I do want to help," she said. "I'm just not sure how much I should expose Rae to."

"Expose me to what, Mom?"

Rae's voice behind Frankie startled her. She

turned and saw her daughter wearing her periwinkle one-piece bathing suit. Her eyes looked soft and a bit unfocused, the way they always did when she didn't wear her glasses.

"What are you and Ben talking about?"

## Chapter Six

"Nothing, Rae," Frankie reassured her daughter. "We weren't talking about anything important at all. Ben's just leaving, and you and I are going to the beach."

She wondered if she was being honest enough with Rae, but her natural inclination was—and always had been—to protect her.

At every stage, Rae had been small for her age and that, combined with her endearing disheveled awkwardness, could make her seem younger than she was. But, as her mother, Frankie also knew that there was a part of her daughter that was thoughtful and sharply observant, and it occurred to her that Rae probably had her own thoughts and questions about the vandalism and it might be a good idea to talk about it.

Rae, with her troubled face, was still waiting for an answer.

"We were just talking about some of the things that have been going on in town," Frankie confessed, deciding on the straightforward approach. "But I don't want you to ruin your time here worrying about it. It will all work out."

She leaned down and gently adjusted one of Rae's lopsided bathing suit straps. When she stood up again, she found that she couldn't quite meet Ben's eyes.

"Have fun at the beach, ladies," he said lightly. "Rae, if you have time later and your mom says that it's okay, I think Dad has a new puzzle you could help him with."

"Maybe I can," Rae said softly, "if Mom says."

"Yes, that would be fine," Frankie said.

"How did things go at the library?" Ben asked "Did you have fun, Rae?"

She nodded. After a small hesitation, she said with a giggle, "My mom said that you went for a swim."

"Oh, did she now?"

Frankie tried to stifle her own smile, but she gave in to it when Ben's eyes twinkled at her above Rae's head.

When Rae decided she'd better make one more trip to the bathroom before they left for the beach, Ben said quickly in a lowered tone, "I hope Rae isn't too nervous about what's been going on. I'd hate it if it ruined your summer. I didn't mean her to overhear anything that would make her uncomfortable."

"It's okay," Frankie said. "It's probably better if I talk about it openly with her. She's getting older. I have to remember that. Maybe we'll see you and Al down at the beach later."

Ben left then, just before Rae came out.

"Did Ben go?" she asked.

"Yes," Frankie said. "But he might bring his dad down to the beach later if he'll come."

Rae shifted a bit and then blurted out, "If you think something really bad is going to happen, Mom, I wish you'd just tell me."

Frankie suddenly felt the urge to pray more strongly than she had in a long time. Even if she wasn't sure God would answer, she thought it might just feel good to voice all of her confusion and concerns.

"Oh, Rae, I wouldn't keep you here if I thought that."

"Okay," Rae said. She studied her feet and then added in a voice so faint that Frankie had to strain to hear it, "I don't like it when you and Ben talk about things that you won't tell me about."

\* \* \*

Back in his cabin, Ben was thinking about his conversation with Frankie when he heard a crash come from the room his Dad slept in and a muffled exclamation.

"Are you okay, Dad? What happened?" Ben called. He left the coffee he'd been making and took three quick strides to the bedroom.

Inside the room, Al looked both befuddled and defensive, pointing at a toppled dresser. It didn't take much detective work to figure out that he had opened all of the drawers, starting at the bottom, until it was unbalanced and had tipped over.

Ben's stomach spontaneously clenched in frustration, but he reminded himself of what he owed his father and, with a prayer and some effort, brought his impatience under control.

When they had moved to this cabin, Ben had tried to help Al unpack his suitcase and put his items into the dresser drawers. But his father had balked so intensely that he had quickly decided that it wasn't worth the tussle and had left Al to rummage through his suitcase each day for what he wanted to wear. And that led to another matter.

Despite the hot weather, Al insisted on dressing every day in his favourite pair of full-length pants, a long-sleeved shirt and shoes and socks. Again, though, Ben had soon learned that it wasn't worth the battle. The regulars who had been visiting Silver Lake for years knew Al and Ben and were sympathetic. As for the weekend crowd, often made up of carousing teenagers and office workers who were more than ready for some lazy lounging, there wasn't much he could do about their questioning and critical stares, so he chose to ignore them.

Ben sighed. It really would be good to have someone to talk to about these kinds of things, and once again he thought of Frankie and, for a brief moment, he allowed himself to consider the impossible: how good it would feel to talk to someone, not only about his father's disease but about everything. Oh, he knew that God knew, but somehow that wasn't the same—and he wondered if that was what the Lord was trying to tell him.

Ben righted the dresser and helped put his dad's scattered belongings back into his suitcase, with Al watching intently and pointing vigorously to make sure things went back the way he wanted. No sooner was that done than Al began pacing and insisted, "Let's go!"

There were moments like this when summer's end loomed with immediacy and yet could also seem too far away as Ben pondered the enormity of the days ahead of him, watching his father crumble piece by piece into a strange, unmanageable creature.

Ben suggested to his dad that they walk down to the beach and stop by the old playground that had kept Ben entertained for many hours when he was a boy. He thought his dad might like that. They could also stop in the Beachfront Confectionery and get a couple of the sausage rolls his father enjoyed. If they happened to run into Frankie and Rae, so be it.

He knelt in front of his father, tugged his socks straight and tied his shoes. Al grumbled and swatted at the top of Ben's head.

"Please don't do that, Dad," Ben said.

As they walked past the shops and the gas station to the path that led down to the beach, Ben caught bits of conversation about the latest attack of vandalism and speculation on what was going to happen next. He glanced sideways at his father, who ambled beside him, sweat already showing on his long-sleeved shirt, with his eyes straight ahead. In the past, Al would have been one of the first people to encourage others not to give in to fear and dismay, but now he scarcely seemed aware of what was going on around him.

Maybe, Ben thought, it was time for him to step up and take on that role—rally the troops, as it were. Would that help him finally feel worthy to fill his father's shoes?

He doubted it.

When they got to the beach, Ben tried to elicit in his father some memory connected to the playground.

"Look, Dad," he said, giving one of the swings a gentle push. "How many hours do you think we spent here while Mom went shopping, eh?"

It didn't surprise him, although it still saddened him, when his dad didn't respond. Ben kept talking despite the lack of reply. He thought that no one knew for sure just how much people with the disease understood. Besides, sometimes it felt good simply to say things out loud.

"How many talks do you think we had here about God and about where my life was going? I'm glad you never gave up on me, Dad. I don't know if I ever told you that…"

But Al's attention was riveted in another direction.

"That girl," he said, pointing.

Ben's eyes followed the direction of where his Dad's finger pointed and he spotted Rae, who had obviously been in the lake for a dip and was now diligently pushing sand into some kind of construction. Almost instinctively, his eyes sought out Frankie. He smiled when he spotted her, wearing an oversize straw sun hat and busily scribbling in a notebook of some kind.

Al bolted in their direction, and Ben stumbled and stubbed his toe on a tree branch as he hurried to catch up.

Rae looked up first as they approached and raised a hand to shade her eyes as she squinted into the sun.

"Careful of my mermaid," she cautioned. Ben looked and could indeed see the scales Rae was sculpting onto a long, curving tail.

"Hey, that's really good," he said, and the little girl shrugged shyly.

His father crouched down beside Rae, and soon the two of them were busily engaged with the sand creation. Ben lowered himself onto the sand, a little distance from Frankie. He wrapped his arms around his knees and looked out at the water, not sure he should interrupt her writing. He couldn't deny that he was curious about what she was doing.

Frankie set aside her notebook and also looked out at the water, feigning indifference. Despite her efforts not to be, she was all too aware of Ben's physical presence and it distracted her from the thoughts she had been trying to form. That was precisely the kind of thing she had to avoid if she wanted to be a strong, independent woman forging ahead on her own terms.

But if life was fair, she grumbled to herself, he wouldn't be getting perfectly bronzed by the sun while she burrowed under some straw monstrosity in an attempt to avoid burning, peeling and sprouting another enthusiastic crop of freckles.

It was good to see Rae and Al busy together, and Ben probably appreciated it, too. Not that she had any real inkling of his feelings, but it was only natural that a caregiver was grateful for times to relax and reflect. She had noticed that, in a short space of time, Al was communicating less and frustration stepped up to devour him more quickly. She wondered if Ben noticed it, too. Sometimes, she knew, those closest to the person were the last to see the truth.

It was Ben who finally broke the silence, but he still didn't look in her direction.

"Writing a bestseller?"

Oh, so he had seen her journal, which embarrassed her slightly. After the way her ex-husband had reacted, she wasn't about to tell him about her plans to get a nursing degree, never mind that Ben seemed to be the complete opposite of Trevor.

She, too, kept her eyes on the water and answered, "Just making a list of things I don't want to forget." It was true enough even if she did make it sound like a grocery list.

Silence fell between them again.

Frankie saw that Rae had given Al a handful of pebbles and was showing him how to make a crown for the sand mermaid.

She smiled with quiet pride at the things her daughter paid attention to and looked over at Ben to see if he also noticed that Rae was copying his way of giving Al things to keep him occupied.

Ben caught her look and showed with a nod and a smile that he had seen and understood.

"What else are people saying about what's going on in town?" Frankie asked, not wanting the conversation's focus to go back to her journal. "Does anyone else think it's kids, like you do?"

"I think so," Ben said. "I mean, it seems like the most logical explanation."

Frankie thought about the stark declaration on the side of the Nature Center and shuddered slightly, as she tried to comprehend what kind of kid would write something like that.

"Are you cold?" Ben asked.

"No…just thinking."

"Did you tell Rae more about what we were talking about? She strikes me as a pretty observant kid."

"She is," Frankie said. "Yes, I thought it was better to be frank with her. Not that there's much to tell her so far since no one really knows much yet. But I decided it's best that she hears from me and not overhears it from other people talking."

"That's probably a good idea," Ben agreed.

Frankie swatted away a mosquito that had been circling her ankle with single-minded purposefulness.

"I think she's okay," she continued. "I mean, she was pretty rattled by what happened this morning at the Nature Center, like we all were. Now, though, she's adjusted to the idea of going to the library and actually seems happy about it. I'm trying to not dwell on it and I think she's following my lead."

Ben nodded. "You set a good example for her. It's clear that she looks up to you."

"What choice does she have?" Frankie tried to make a joke out of it because compliments didn't sit easy with her. Her parents were loving, but very practical people who believed in facing life head-on without making a lot of fuss about it, so they never gave praise to see people who, in their minds, were just doing what was expected of them. And Trevor... Well, if she believed him—and she still struggled not to— she couldn't do anything right.

"What will they do if the vandal is a minor?" Frankie asked. "I mean, what will happen to him—or her?"

"I'm not exactly sure," Ben admitted. "I guess it would depend on the circumstances, whether there are previous offenses or not. For some reason, I'm thinking there won't be. It could be placement in a juvenile offender's program or maybe some kind of community service."

"I think that would be better," Frankie said.

"Which? The community service?"

"Yes, because at least that way there is some benefit from it and the person might actually learn something."

"I agree," Ben said. "What kind of community service were you thinking of?"

Frankie cringed away from a horsefly and Ben shooed it off.

When the slight disturbance was over she answered, "We have something at the care home where I work that seems to bring really good results. It's a youth-senior pairing."

"Sounds interesting," Ben said. "What's that all about?"

"Young people who might not have the greatest family life or have been in trouble of some kind get paired with seniors who don't get many visitors and are lonely, or who need help doing things. Some unexpected and really good friendships have grown out of it, and everyone feels more worthwhile and not just lost in the shuffle."

"Interesting," Ben said again, rubbing his chin.

"Mom?" Rae was at her side then, with Al a step behind her. "Did you see our mermaid?"

"I did and she's absolutely beautiful. Come here, you!" Frankie pulled Rae in for a hug, enjoying the coolness of her damp body and the smell of her sunscreen and the warm, grainy sand.

Rae flopped like a rag doll for a few seconds, leaning on her mother, and giggled when Frankie gasped at the damp suit touching her skin on her bare legs. Then she straightened up and acknowledged Ben with a quick look.

"Your dad is talking about church," she informed him. "He wants to go."

"Ah, okay. Church is one of the things he remembers the best," Ben explained. "He feels at home and he'll always sit peacefully there. So," he admitted, "it's good for both of us."

"Church," Al echoed. "Yep, let's go to that place."

"In a few days," Ben promised. "It's not Sunday today, Dad."

"Where do you go?" Rae asked, "I haven't seen a church here."

"There's a Bible camp just a few miles from here," Ben said, "and they have services. It's really a great little place, although sometimes birds fly in and we get the occasional squirrel, too. Usually afterward, they serve hamburgers and hot dogs and have ice cream."

"Squirrels at church?" Rae said, her eyes wide. "Mom, can we go?"

"You'd be more than welcome," Ben encouraged.

Frankie didn't know what to say. The last thing she wanted to do was go to church. But Rae had always enjoyed Sunday school, and, although she hadn't said anything all this time, she must be missing it, Frankie realized.

As if sensing her mom's thoughts, Rae pushed a bit harder. "Mom, I like church and we haven't gone in such a long time."

Surely, she could do this one small thing for her daughter, despite her own feelings. What was an hour or so on a Sunday in the whole scheme of things? But was she really just doing it for Rae, or was there something more that tugged at her?

## Chapter Seven

Ben had not expected the jolt he got when Frankie agreed to attend church with him. It had taken him a long time, a very long time, to feel as if his inside relationship with God finally matched what he showed on the outside. To have someone at church with him, he thought, would be such a personal, revealing thing. He suspected that Frankie's faith was shaky at best, and he was curious about whether the service would touch her in any way. He was fully aware that she was attending for Rae's sake; it seemed there was hardly anything she wouldn't do for that little girl. His heart stuttered when he thought of Frankie's unselfishness in that regard.

Now that it was Sunday morning, though, he was preoccupied by his attempts to get some food into his father so that he wouldn't complain of hunger halfway through the service, and also with trying to find them both clean shirts to wear.

As well, his mind was occupied with thoughts of the continued vandalism. It frustrated him that people had many opinions to express but could shed no new light on the matter.

Besides all of that, curiosity about Frankie and what her story was played a soft, persistent melody in the back of his mind.

*Be with her and Rae, Lord. Help them through whatever challenges they are facing.* Because he had no doubt they were struggling.

"How's breakfast, Dad?" He had made his dad's toast slightly burnt, the way Al liked it, and lightly spread with peanut butter and raspberry jelly.

Al glowered at him but continued to chew and didn't throw his toast on the floor, which Ben took as a positive sign.

"We're going to church," Ben reminded him, when Al balked at getting dressed.

Fortunately, the word had the impact he wanted it to. Almost instantly, Al grew calmer and allowed his son to help him into his shirt and do up the buttons. Ben then got dressed himself in a light blue dress shirt and navy dress pants.

"Okay, we can do this," Ben said, giving himself a little pep talk. "We're not going to be late."

If he was honest with himself, he knew he wouldn't mind being a bit late if it was just going to be him and his dad. The camp church was a welcoming place, where they always saw familiar faces, and it wasn't likely anything would come to a grinding halt as they waited for Ben and Al to make an entrance.

No, he knew he was nervous in a way that he wouldn't have been if his summer neighbors hadn't been going with them.

Ben had suggested that they all ride in one car, which Frankie reluctantly agreed to after he convinced her it would be easier that way.

When Ben and Al came out of their cabin, Frankie and Rae were sitting on their deck waiting.

Ben noted that Rae looked cute in her pink-and-blue-plaid sundress, and he wondered with some amusement how long her hair would behave and stay smoothed into its high, swinging ponytail. He guessed not for long.

When he saw Frankie, his amusement sped away and was replaced by a surge of admiration. He thought she looked like a warm summer day, with her hair curling softly on her shoulders, set off by the bright yellow of her dress.

He swallowed and said, "Let's go, Dad. It looks like the ladies are waiting for us."

"Wanna go to church," Al replied.

"You both look very lovely," Ben told them, as he held open the back door of the car for Frankie and Rae.

Rae rewarded him with a shy smile and moved her head to and fro to show him how her ponytail would swing back and forth like a silky pendulum. Frankie gave him a look like he'd said something in a language she didn't understand, and slid into the back seat without a word.

Wordlessly Ben handed her the seat belt, while she in turn helped Rae find hers. Ben ignored Al's swatting hands and got him buckled in and soon they were on their way.

Ben always enjoyed the drive from the beach to Camp Kindling. The tall pine trees that grew abundantly on both sides of the road gave him a feeling of protection—a green secret haven from the turmoil of the world. But Ben found on that particular Sunday morning that they could not shelter him from the turmoil in his mind.

It was a good thing they were on their way to church, he thought, because he needed to be deep in prayer right now.

Rae hopped with excitement in her seat, her ponytail bouncing in time.

"This is so cool," she said when they arrived. "Look, Mom, the church is like a big log cabin. I sure hope some animals come in today. Wouldn't that be cool?"

"Very cool," Frankie agreed.

Ben could see it was an autopilot response and that Frankie's eyes were tinged with uneasiness. He guessed that it had been a while since she'd been at church and was nervous about what might be expected of her. He wanted to reassure her that everything would be fine, but the truth was that he knew there would be plenty of curiosity and questions about them being there together.

They arrived as the worship team ended one song and launched into another and quietly slid into the back row. Ben encouraged Frankie and Rae to go into the bench seat first, so that he could be with his father on the aisle, in case Al wouldn't sit still.

But the atmosphere of music and familiar scripture passages and prayer worked to soothe Al as it always did, and Ben was able to enjoy the sermon, which was about Paul's affliction and God's strength being made perfect in his weakness. With Rae sitting between them, he couldn't see Frankie's face or gauge her reaction to the sermon.

The hour or so went by quickly and he wondered how eager Frankie would be to make a getaway. Rae was tugging at her hands with a plea to stay for a hot dog and, after what seemed to Ben like a lengthy hesitation, Frankie said yes. He guessed it was at that point she wished she had brought her own car.

During the service, Ben had allowed himself the luxury of forgetting how curious a church family could be: kindhearted, yes, well-meaning, indeed, but human and, along with that, at times all too curious. He didn't have time to prepare Frankie before clusters of women he had known for years spotted them and zeroed in.

May Watkins had finally stopped pinching his cheeks when he was twenty-four and had gathered the gumption to ask her not to. Still, somehow, Ben always felt that pinch in her intense gaze.

"Ben Cedar!" she exclaimed. "And here we thought you were playing hooky this morning, didn't we, girls?"

Deb Forrester, Wyn Hoffert and Marybeth Merasty bobbed their heads in unison like a choir on a fact-finding mission. He always thought, with some amusement, that they looked like they belonged to some kind of club that urged them to sport the same short hairstyles and to peer through their glasses in the same bright, inquisitive way.

"Oh no, I wouldn't do that," Ben said, his tone mild, his thoughts racing on how to do the impossible. How could he keep their attention off Frankie and Rae? He could only imagine how Frankie would feel about being hit with a barrage of questions and it wouldn't be good.

"It's nice to see you, Al," Marybeth said. "You're looking dapper this morning."

Maybe that was his opening. "Dad and I thank you, ladies," Ben chimed in, as his father's face was rearranging itself in such a way that looked like his response might not be quite as polite. "I think Dad's hungry and we'd better get in line for those hamburgers and hot dogs before the lines get too long."

"Not hungry!" Al said, naturally choosing that particular moment to verbalize his thoughts in an unmistakable manner.

"Oh, let's head over there together," Wyn said briskly but kindly. "You might change your mind, Al, by the time we get through the lineup." She walked beside his father, steering him gently by placing her fingers lightly on his wrist. To Ben's relief, he didn't protest, and he was grateful for these women who had known him and his father for so many years, who had been around for some of his own less stellar ones and who still wanted to help.

His feeling of relief passed quickly when, behind him, he heard May say to Frankie, "I can't tell you how good it is to finally see Ben with a lovely young woman."

He didn't dare turn around to see May smile while her eyes blazed with a hundred questions. Most of all, he didn't dare see the look on Frankie's face.

Then, somewhere in him, that tweak of amusement took over the way it did at the strangest times, and he once again gave a grudging nod to God's sense of humor. He found himself perking his ears to see how Frankie would answer.

Ladies at church, Frankie thought. They were the same everywhere you went. But, to her surprise, there was no malice in the thought. On the surface, the ladies might fit into some stereotypical mold, but she was sure they were capable of depth and unexpected empathy.

Memories she had pushed to the back of her mind because she had needed to disconnect herself from church came rushing back, and one in particular: a lady from her church, who she had long viewed as being prim, always in control and rather judgmental, was the first to visit after Trevor left, and had astonished Frankie with her account of her own failed marriage.

Frankie realized she was willing to chat with

these ladies, especially if it gave her an opportunity to find out more about Ben. She quelled
her inner arguments before they had a chance to
fully surface. Just because she never intended to
be in a relationship again didn't mean that she
couldn't be curious about someone. She just had
to make sure she steered the conversation away
from her and onto what they knew about him.

They exchanged names and shook hands.
The ladies cooed over Rae, who was at her en-
dearingly awkward best, ducking her head and
scratching a nonexistent mosquito bite before
making a run for it to join Ben and Al in line
for food.

Frankie watched and willed good manners
onto her daughter as the woman who stood in
line with them apparently found Rae's cheeks
irresistibly pinch-able. To her credit, Rae stood
her ground, but Frankie stifled a laugh when
she saw her small jaw lock into place and had
no doubt that Rae was doing some inward eye
rolling.

"So, how long *have* you known Ben?" the one
named Deb asked.

"Oh, we really don't know each other,"
Frankie returned smoothly. "Our cabins just
happen to be across the road from each other
at Silver Lake and he was kind enough to offer
us a ride when my daughter wanted to go to

church this morning." She hoped the fact that she hadn't said that she wanted to go to church would slip by them.

"Oh…so you're not a couple then?" Marybeth chimed in. "We saw you together and we honestly thought…"

They looked so forlorn that, for a moment, Frankie wished that she could tell them that she and Ben were in a relationship. Instead, she briefly relayed the account of their arrival at the cabins and how Ben had offered to trade cabins with them, even though they were strangers.

"That sounds like Ben." Wyn nodded sagely. She added something that tweaked Frankie's curiosity. "That boy has come a long way."

Frankie wanted to ask more about that, but the conversation turned to the vandalism. They all agreed it was puzzling and disturbing.

"Um, the woman with Ben and Al and my daughter is trying to get your attention," Frankie said, as she noticed her peering back at them with her forefinger and one eyebrow raised in question.

"That's May," Wyn said, as Deb grimaced slightly and gave her head one brief shake.

Frankie watched May's face collapse into disconcertment. Clearly, she had not received the answer she'd hoped for.

"We're sorry if we've overstepped our boundaries," Deb said. "We've known Ben for years and, well, we've seen him go through some tough times, is the truth of it. But he's come out the other side and he's made us all proud. The way that boy takes care of his father…"

"Plus, we saw the way he looked at you," Wyn put in, "and we were sure there was something…"

"We just hoped there was," Marybeth affirmed, "because he deserves someone to share the ups and downs of life with. The way he acts sometimes, you'd think he was responsible for the whole world, but he needs someone to be there for him, whether he admits it or not."

Frankie smiled weakly as she inwardly wondered what they meant by the way Ben looked at her. It made her uncomfortable so she changed the subject by saying that it had been a good church service. Somewhat to her surprise, as she said it, she realized that she meant it, though she didn't know if she would ever be a regular churchgoer again.

All the chitchat made the line move quickly, and soon Frankie had her own hamburger, which was slightly burnt but in the delicious way that grilled hamburgers can be. She stopped at a table to put mustard and relish and a slice of cheese on it, added a scoop of coleslaw to the side of her plate, then scanned the group to find Rae.

She located her, sitting beside Al at one of the picnic tables, happily munching her hot dog, which was no doubt doused in ketchup. Frankie shuddered slightly at Rae's culinary tastes.

Frankie and the other women found room on the opposite side of the table, and she found herself sitting directly across from Ben.

"I hope the ladies here haven't been ruining my reputation," he said. His tone was light, but his eyes searched hers, asking real questions.

The intensity in his blue eyes made Frankie's heart quicken, but she pushed a bantering tone into her reply.

"Oh, we just got past all the hearts you broke in your youth, and we were about to move on to your illustrious career as a bank robber."

"What do you mean 'in my youth'?" Ben protested. "I'm still in my youth!"

"Well, compared to Methuselah maybe…"

Chuckles broke out around the table and Frankie couldn't help enjoying the look of humorous surprise on Ben's face.

"Well, he's still plenty young," May pointed out, "as are you. And he sure could have been a heartbreaker if other things didn't take up his time. I can't for the life of me figure out why you never found a nice woman and settled down, Ben."

The note of lightness fled the table, and Frankie felt her invisible wall locking into place again.

Unmindful, May carried on. "I couldn't help getting my hopes up when I saw the two of you come in together with your little girl." Her gaze landed on Frankie. "I have no doubt that Ben would make an excellent father, and I really don't think that the Lord means for any of us to be alone…"

"I have a dad!" The wounded words flew from Rae's mouth. Frankie hadn't been sure she was paying attention, but now she knew with grim certainty that her daughter had been listening.

"I have a dad! I do! And I don't need another one!"

Rae untucked herself from the picnic table, then ran as fast as she could away from the table.

## Chapter Eight

For a moment, Ben was stymied. Then he sprang into action, going after Frankie as she chased after Rae. Fortunately, Rae was wearing flip-flops and hadn't made much progress. He caught up with both of them with minimal effort.

He directed his words to Rae. "Rae, I know May didn't mean to upset you and I'm sorry that she did. Sometimes people speak without thinking. Won't you come finish your hot dog? I know my dad loves your company and I'm sure May would like to apologize herself."

Rae bowed her head, twisting her foot around her opposite leg and whispered, "S'okay." Then she lifted her head and said, hoarsely but a bit louder, "It's okay, but I'm just going to stay here with my mom for a minute."

Ben's heart went out to her. Rae was such

a sensitive, reserved little girl, and he suspected she was embarrassed over her outburst. He wished he could tell her that he understood more than she and her mother realized what it felt like to lose control.

He dared to look at Frankie then. She returned his gaze, but appeared distant and closed off again.

"If I had my way," he told her, "we would have stayed far away from a conversation like that. I'm sure you feel exactly the same."

Frankie gave her acknowledgment with a brief nod and a rather grim smile, then knelt on the ground, unmindful of getting her dress dusty, and spoke to Rae in a low, gentle tone. Ben couldn't hear the words, but eventually Rae's face grew less distressed and she nodded slowly. Frankie stood up and offered Rae her hand and, together, they headed back to the picnic table.

Back at the table, earnest conversations were clearly in progress, with a great deal of head nodding and then some smiles, which told him that things had been settled to everybody's satisfaction.

Except, for reasons he couldn't quite figure out, his own.

Just then, Frankie caught his eye and offered an apologetic smile. There was an expression in her deep brown eyes like she somehow understood how he was feeling even if he didn't fully understand it himself.

But before he could determine if Frankie really did understand or if he was just seeing what he wanted to see, Al began to make noises of protest and turned his empty plate over.

With hurried excuses and declarations that it had been great to see them again, Ben got Al up from the table as quickly as possible before his restlessness turned to increased agitation.

As he hurried his father away, he could hear May start feeling her way back into a conversation with Frankie. He didn't have to be there to know that her motives were crystal clear.

He heard Frankie say in a way that was polite yet unmistakably firm, "Thank you for welcoming us to your church and for all your interest and hospitality. I think that Rae and I will excuse ourselves now and explore this lovely camp."

The funny, wonderful thing was, Ben thought, was that if he closed his eyes, he could absolutely picture the way her face would look when she said it—direct gaze, polite smile locked into place.

"Did you like your hot dog?" Rae asked Al, as she and Frankie caught up with them. "Mine was really good!"

He smiled and put his hand on her head. "Ketchup," he said.

"I liked the sermon," Frankie said to Ben, and by the way she said it, he knew that she was making a peace offering, letting him know that she didn't blame him for what had happened.

"The minister's a good speaker," Ben agreed. "I've heard him a couple of times before and he's easy to follow and understand. They don't have the same one here every Sunday," he explained. "There are various ones from around the area that take turns."

"Did your dad ever preach out here?" Frankie asked.

"Yes, and he loved it."

They walked quietly beside each other, enjoying the beautiful scenery around them.

Frankie waited to see if Ben would elaborate on his dad's experiences at the camp, but he seemed content to just walk. She guessed that they were both glad to have a break from the chatter at the table. She thought about some of the things that had come up in her conversation with the ladies and curiosity niggled at her until she couldn't help saying, "One of the ladies said that you'd come a long way…"

She saw Ben's posture stiffen and regretted her words almost as soon as they had escaped her mouth. Yet, she wanted to hear how he would answer—*if* he would answer.

"Haven't we all come a long way, one way or another?" he said, turning to her with an unreadable expression.

"I didn't mean…"

"It's okay," Ben said. "It's in the past and I just don't talk about it much."

Frankie waited.

"I guess you could just say I was a typical PK—preacher's kid," Ben said. "I felt I had to prove I was my own person, and in trying to do that, I made some not-so-great choices." He shrugged. "That's about it."

Something in his eyes belied the casual tone of his voice. Frankie sensed there was a lot more to the story, but she didn't want to push.

Besides, what good would it do to know or to get involved?

Ahead of them, Rae stopped and bent over to pick up a feather, then scampered after Al to show it to him. He took it and studied it, then tickled her under the chin with it.

"Kids are always drawn to Dad," Ben remarked as if, Frankie thought, he was happy to change the subject.

"Rae really likes him," she agreed.

"I love it out here," Ben said, after they had walked for a little while longer in silence. "I can really feel God's presence here." He glanced over at Frankie. "But I don't think you're a big fan of the God talk, are you?"

"I can handle a bit of it," Frankie said.

"Well, thank you for saying so," Ben said. His face relaxed into a grin. "Looks like we've found ourselves on a walk with Dad again," he said. "I wonder how many miles we could log just following him around."

"I don't mind," Frankie said. "It's beautiful here and that's the great thing about being on vacation—we don't have to be locked into a schedule."

"True enough. Good attitude!"

"Why don't you show us where you stayed when you were here," she suggested. She added, teasingly, "And tell us about all those broken hearts."

"Hey!" Ben protested laughingly. "It was you who started that rumor, not me."

Then his eyes darkened again in that compelling way they did and he said, "But I bet you've broken a few hearts in your lifetime."

For a moment Frankie savored the long-forgotten sensation that a compliment like that could give someone, but then the irony of it hit her with full force.

What would Ben think if he knew the truth

about her? He would probably feel sorry for her and she didn't think she could stand that.

Still, she mused, he had shared something about himself, however sparingly, and she supposed she could do the same. She heard the frosty tone of warning in her own voice that indicated he was not to push for details as she said shortly, "I'm divorced. I'm hardly the heart-breaking type."

She watched an array of expressions pass over Ben's face. Curiosity, yes, but more than that, Frankie realized, there was compassion and understanding.

"That must have been tough," he said simply, softly. To her surprise, he draped his arm around her and drew her against him. Frankie automatically stiffened, but even as she did so, she knew there was nothing untoward in his gesture. It was meant to comfort and bolster her, and the realization of how much she needed that hit her like a sudden punch and made her feel off-kilter. She closed her eyes and allowed herself to lean into him, feeling the strong arm that sheltered her and breathing in the clean, masculine smell of him.

"Mom?" Rae called out, running back toward them. "Ben?"

Frankie gasped and quickly wriggled out from under Ben's arm. For a few seconds, Rae had slipped her mind. She couldn't afford to be careless like that. It was dangerous for her to let her emotions take over, and she resolved even more firmly that it wouldn't happen again.

What had Rae seen? What would she think and how would she explain it to her?

But it was soon apparent that Rae had more pressing matters on her mind.

"What is it, Rae?" Frankie asked, hoping her emotional turmoil wasn't in her voice.

Rae looked at her, glanced anxiously at Ben, looked at her feet and, with a blush spreading from her neck upward, told her secret to the ground.

"Pardon me, Rae?" Ben asked gently. "We couldn't quite hear you."

"I said," Rae repeated, wrought with misery, "Al stomped on my feather and said a bad word."

## Chapter Nine

It felt like a huge, invisible hand had reached in, yanked Ben out of the hazy, speculative dream world he'd been residing in and dumped him unceremoniously back into reality.

One minute he had been enjoying the warm coconut and balsam scent of Frankie's hair, and the next he was being reminded, in no uncertain terms, that this wasn't the right time for distractions like that, and, he thought, nearly buckling over for a moment with acute regret, there probably wouldn't be a right time. Ever.

"Did he hurt you?" he asked Rae in a rather urgent tone.

She shook her head emphatically and looked startled at the question.

He looked over to check on his father, who stood where Rae had left him. Al smiled and waved at his son.

Ben sighed and waved back as he reminded himself that Dad couldn't help it, and if he had been aware that he had upset Rae, he would have felt very badly and immediately tried to make amends.

Then again, if his dad was himself, nothing like that would have happened in the first place. Not for the first time, Ben thought that Alzheimer's was an utterly cruel disease, turning loved ones into unrecognizable people.

He thought they would have the summer together, but if things had regressed to the point that his father would lash out at an innocent little girl like that...

*Please Lord, I'm not ready. Help me make the right decision for Dad. Help me to do what's best, and, more than anything, help me to know what that is.*

He heard Frankie explaining to Rae that the disease sometimes made people say and do things that were entirely out of character, things they would never want to say or do if they weren't sick.

"Al couldn't help it any more than you can help being sick when you have the flu."

Rae nodded, a wise expression on her face. "You mean the words just rushed right out of his stomach, don't you?"

Ben watched Frankie smile, and his heart

filled with gratitude for her understanding of the disease and for her compassion. Although she had revealed little, he sensed that she had been through a lot. Yet, she always pulled herself together and was the mother that Rae needed her to be. He felt his admiration for her growing.

So, who then, he found himself wondering, would be there to be strong for Frankie when she needed someone? He prayed that the Father who sees and knows all hearts would reach her in some way.

"Let's go!" Al had joined them again and was clearly anxious to continue the walk.

*Is Rae okay?* Ben silently mouthed to Frankie, his eyebrows raised in a question.

She nodded.

"Thank you," Ben said, as they started walking again.

"For what?"

He could tell that Frankie was trying to distance herself again.

"For understanding my dad and for explaining it to Rae." Ben hesitated. "We all need extra support at times and if you ever want to talk about—"

"I don't," Frankie cut him off. "I understand your dad because of my job, and I will always help Rae understand and get through things. I'm her mom."

Ben saw her make small fists at her side and then release them. He guessed it was a way she had of releasing tension.

"Has Al had many outbursts?" she asked in a clinical way. It was clear to Ben that she wanted the conversation far away from her feelings and needs.

"Some," he admitted. "So far, they've mostly been around me. He hasn't done *that* around other people, especially not around kids. He really likes Rae, at least as far as I can tell."

A picture came to his mind of the tremulous little girl clinging to her mom's hand.

"I hope she knows that," Ben said, "and that this doesn't set her back."

"Rae will be fine," Frankie said briskly. "I'll make sure of that."

"I've no doubt you will."

They continued to walk.

"Anyway," Ben continued after a moment or two of silence, "it makes me realize that I'm probably only kidding myself if I think I can keep him out of a home much longer."

At this declaration, he saw something in Frankie visibly soften again. Her shoulders relaxed, and finally she looked directly at him with sympathy in her eyes.

Frankie said, "I've had people tell me that the day they had to put their loved one into a care facility was the hardest day of their lives, even more so than when the person passed away."

Ben nodded. "I miss the person Dad used to be so much it's like I've already been through a grieving process of sorts."

It was guilt, too, he added silently. He couldn't speak for anyone else, but for him it was the terrible burden of guilt that came with trying to be the kind of son he should have been when his parents could have appreciated it.

"Yes, I've heard people say similar things," Frankie said.

"How do people do it, then?" Ben asked. "How do they finally decide that, despite how horrible it feels, it's the only choice left?"

"I think that's your answer right there," Frankie said. "It becomes obvious when it's the only choice left. The person becomes a danger to themselves or others, or you just know in your very bones that you don't have a drop left to give without harming yourself. Sometimes…" She hesitated, and a look of pain and distaste crossed her face.

"What?"

"Well, sometimes caregivers don't pay enough attention to their own warning signs and so much builds up that they can become abusive."

"I'd never let that happen," Ben said grimly. He'd made some unwise choices at times, but he knew he could trust himself in that.

"I doubt anyone ever thinks that they would."

"You've given me some things to think about," he said.

"Aren't you…"

Ben could see that Frankie was puzzling over how to phrase her question, but he didn't know why.

"Aren't you— I mean, haven't you ever prayed about it?"

Ah, so that was it, Ben thought. She wasn't sure if she should ask him if he prayed because that might mean she was admitting God was there.

Out loud he said simply, "All the time."

Slightly ahead of them, Rae and Al walked some distance from each other. They kept their eyes focused on the ground, occasionally exchanging furtive glances. No doubt, Rae was trying to ease herself back into feeling completely comfortable with Al. Who knew what his father thought, though Ben doubted that he had any recollection of the outburst that had shocked Rae.

Ben looked over at Frankie to point the two of them out to her, and he saw that she was already looking in their direction with a thoughtful face.

It occurred to him how often they noticed the same things at the same time, and a thought prodded that if things were different, it might be fun to explore that. But there was no sense dwelling on that. He made himself lighten his tone and said, "So, you wanted to see all the places that molded me into the marvellous man I am today?"

Frankie rolled her eyes, but not without a small smile.

"I guess I have nothing better to do," she retorted.

"Ouch!" Ben cringed jokingly and made a gesture like he was stabbing himself in the heart. "Now there's a ringing endorsement."

As they toured the cabins that all had names like Wolf's Teeth and Bear Claw, Frankie tried to picture the boy that Ben had been when he was here. She thought about the preacher's-kid comment he had made and she wondered if he had naturally fit in here or had had to struggle to do so. And what would he have been willing to do to erase those barriers? But those idle speculations were far from being the only thing on her mind.

She had smoothed over Rae's reaction to Al because she hadn't wanted to make the situation more difficult than it already was. In reality, though, she was concerned about the effect Al's outburst would have on Rae, especially since she was just coming out of her shell again. She also wondered what impact it would have on Ben and felt like he had some very tough decisions ahead of him.

"Are you bored already?" Ben asked her. "Should I amp up the witty anecdotes?"

He was teasing, but Frankie could see that he was honestly checking up on her, too. She wondered how long her thoughts had been adrift.

She noticed that Al had made himself at home on one of the upper bunks.

"I bet everyone fought over those," Frankie said, pointing.

"I didn't. I'm scared of heights."

From the overly solemn look on Ben's face, she knew he was joking.

"Well, you've been in the church and you saw the dining hall when we picked up burgers," Ben said. "Is there anything else you can think of that you'd like to see?"

"No, I can't think of anything, but thanks. We should probably get back. It was interesting to get a glimpse into your past."

"Maybe someday I'll get a glimpse into yours."

On some level, Frankie understood that Ben had only meant to respond in kind, but since she had told him she was divorced, the words took on an importance that made her uneasy. She could almost sense Ben's inward cringe. Apparently, the words hadn't sounded good to him either once they had left his mouth.

"I really didn't mean that the way it came out," he said.

"I understand," Frankie said.

"I just meant maybe you could tell me if you'd ever been a Girl Scout and gone camping yourself—that kind of thing."

"I know."

If she knew, Frankie asked herself, why was she shutting him out again? Because, she answered her questioning voice, there's no point in letting him in. Even so, she relented and said, "I was never a Girl Scout, but I went to day camp once."

"Day camp?" Ben made an incredulous face. "How can you even make the comparison?"

"You do the same activities like hikes and crafts, and go swimming."

Ben snorted. "It's not camping if you sleep at home."

"Well, it's like camping."

"Hardly."

"Well, we had the same kinds of activities."

Finally, they reached Ben's car.

"Mom?" Rae asked, looking from one to the other. "Are you and Ben having an argument?"

The anxious question stopped Frankie short. How many times had her daughter heard her bicker with her ex-husband about what they spent money on or how late he had come home? She had tried to shelter Rae from as much of it as she could, but their house wasn't large and she always worried that Rae heard more than she wanted her to.

Now, it seemed that her worries were correct.

"No, Sweet Pea," Frankie answered. "We're just having a difference of opinion. How did you like the camp?" she asked, changing the subject. "Do you think you'd ever like to go to camp?"

Rae's furrowed brow lifted a bit. "I think so. I liked going to church at camp."

Rae had always liked church and Frankie knew that it probably wasn't fair to keep her away from it because of her own struggles. She shoved the thought to the back of her mind. She had enjoyed the service, more than she'd expected to, but that didn't mean she was ready to jump back in with both feet.

Ben got Al settled into his seat and buckled in. Al swatted at his hands again, but without much energy, and before they were back on the highway again, he was fast asleep and snoring vigorously.

Rae put her hands over her mouth and giggled. She had accepted that what had come out briefly wasn't really Al, and Frankie breathed a sigh of relief.

"You okay back there?" Ben asked. "Comfy? Is the air-conditioning good?"

"It's good, thanks," Frankie said.

"Great, just let me know if you need anything."

In another mile, Rae also drifted off, her head bouncing lightly off and on Frankie's shoulder.

"Evidently, we're not the world's most interesting company," Ben remarked.

"Apparently not."

"If we'd known, you could have sat up front with me."

For whatever reason, the words made Frankie blush a little, and she was glad that she was in the back seat.

"It's not a long ride," she said.

"Confession time?" Ben asked.

"What?" Frankie said warily.

"It's going to sound selfish, but I wish Dad wouldn't sleep in the car, because it means he might not sleep later, and I count on those times to—well just to *be*?"

From her vantage point in the back seat, Frankie could see only the back of Ben's head and his profile, but somehow, for a split second, she felt she could suddenly see how alone and scared he felt sometimes. She answered as softly as if she was reassuring Rae about something.

"No, not selfish—human."

She thought she could see a line of tension leave his shoulders.

"So," he said, after a minute or two of silence, "you enjoyed yourself today?"

It was funny, Frankie thought, that he didn't like things focused on him any more than she liked to be the focus. And he didn't like to admit when he needed help... They had more in common than she would have guessed at first.

"I did," she agreed. "The camp has the kind of peaceful feel to it that I had hoped for Silver Lake. Silver Lake is lovely, it's just that..."

Ben nodded. She could see the edge of his mouth set in a firm line.

"It was like that," he said. "It should be like that, but all of the vandalism has scarred that."

"Time for my own confession?" Frankie asked.

"Go for it."

"I'm mostly focused on giving Rae as good a holiday as I possibly can, because we don't get these opportunities very often. But, the truth is, I'm so angry and upset that we can't just enjoy ourselves without that looming over our heads. It doesn't seem fair. Just once I'd like to be able to completely relax and trust that things are going to be okay, but every time I think I can…"

Frankie stopped herself when she heard the tremor in her own voice. She didn't cry in front of people, and she certainly wasn't going to start now.

She expected Ben to give her a pat answer about prayer and trust, so his response surprised her.

"I feel the same way. I'm upset about it, too."

"You are?"

Ben didn't answer right away. Al's baritone snore and Rae's softly breathed accompaniment filled the waiting space.

"Of course I am," he finally said. "I don't expect to ever be back here with Dad. I had planned to move him into a care facility at the end of the summer."

His hands clenched the wheel as he directed the car onto the final turn toward Silver Lake. "Now with the way things are—him swearing at Rae and other things—I'm not sure we'll even make it to the end of summer."

Frankie didn't know what upset her more: the potential for more vandalism or the regret that hung on each word out of Ben's mouth, and she was afraid that if it persisted her armor wouldn't stay strong.

# *Chapter Ten*

As Ben struggled to get his father awake and coherent enough to walk into their cabin, he couldn't help feeling slightly envious of Frankie who, despite her own delicate stature, could still carry Rae.

He also noted that it seemed she couldn't get away from him fast enough.

His little pity party didn't help, he mocked himself. As if she didn't have enough to worry about without him adding to it.

Still, he couldn't help feeling that it would be nice, just for once, to tell someone everything he felt and thought about. The strange thing was, Ben couldn't recall ever particularly wanting to do that before he met Frankie. But he was probably just drawn to her because of her knowledge and understanding of their situation, he reminded himself.

He couldn't let himself think it was any more than that.

Meanwhile, Ben was stuck struggling to maneuver his dad out of the front seat of the car. It was a precarious balancing act to awaken his father enough to function but not to get him agitated. Sometimes he woke up in battle mode—that was the worst.

There were times when Ben couldn't remember when his life didn't revolve around seeking the balance between being a good caregiver and not neglecting his own needs. Lately, though, the balance was tipping seriously in the direction of his father, like one of the teeter-totters at the park when all the kids would pile onto one end of it.

He felt guilty for any resentment, even if it was fleeting, because surely this was the least of what he owed his father. He wished for the umpteenth time that his dad could reassure him that everything was forgiven, that he understood his son had had to get away and why he didn't come home as soon as he should have. Of course his dad couldn't, and the voice in his heart on the matter remained devastatingly silent.

Ben didn't dare to imagine the days stretching out ahead of him with the responsibilities piled more and more heavily upon him. Even worse, paradoxically, was thinking about life without his father.

And, in the background, a quiet question lingered in his mind: Just what were his feelings about Frankie?

As if summoned by that very question, Frankie walked out onto her deck, just as Ben managed to maneuver Al into a standing position.

"Nope!" Al protested but without much conviction, so Ben was able to guide him into the cabin and settle him in his bed where, thankfully, he drifted off again.

When he came back outside again, Frankie was still on her deck. She had changed out of the clothes she had worn to church and was wearing shorts, a T-shirt and the baseball cap that had briefly deceived him on that first day. He smiled a little to himself, seeing it. She had confessed on one of their long walks with Al that she had never played the sport, nor did she have any interest in watching it.

"But sunglasses pinch my nose and this keeps the sun out of my eyes."

"They pinch your nose?" he had asked drily.

She had fisted her small hands on her slim hips and glared at him, daring him to provoke her further.

A thought passed through Ben's mind that

she was particularly cute, but he refused to let it nest.

*Lord, don't let me want something when the timing is so bad.*

Frankie had a magazine open on the table, but Ben could see that she wasn't reading, it. She appeared to be deep in thought about something. He didn't want to disturb her and was about to resign himself to tidying around his cabin when she called out softly.

"Did Al go back to sleep?"

"Yes. Is Rae still sleeping?"

"No," Frankie said. "She usually only falls asleep in the car because she closes her eyes so she won't get carsick when she sits in the back seat. She's having some quiet time, though, working on her art project for tomorrow."

"She gets carsick?" Ben asked. "Would she be better off in the front seat?"

"Not if she closes her eyes when she feels it coming on," Frankie explained patiently.

"Hmm, well, okay then."

An unfamiliar sensation washed over Ben as he suddenly wondered what it would be like to be a father, and to be so intimately tied to a child that you knew all those revealing details about them.

Frankie looked pensive, then blurted out, as if she was afraid of changing her mind if she didn't speak right away, "I've got coffee on, if you want some."

"Sure," Ben answered, feeling unexpectedly pleased. He hadn't been sure Frankie would welcome his company after telling him she was divorced. He imagined those words, brief as they were, ripping a hole within her.

Frankie went into her cabin to pour him some coffee and to top up her own.

"Will Al sleep for a while longer, do you think?" she asked, returning to the deck.

Ben shrugged. "Who knows? There's pros and cons if he does. I can relax now, but I'll pay for it later."

"That's exactly how I used to feel with Rae," Frankie agreed.

"Funny the way life goes full circle, isn't it?" Ben commented. But it wasn't the kind of funny that made either of them laugh or even smile.

Ben took a sip of his coffee and glanced at Frankie over the rim of his cup. Her eyes seemed to hold a million secrets in them and he wished, fleetingly, that he could ask. But if he expected her to reveal more, then she might expect the same of him, and he wasn't sure if he was ready for that, now or ever.

"What are you thinking about?" Frankie asked.

Why, Ben wondered, did her radar always zero in on him when he least wanted it to?

He hesitated. It wasn't likely that he could put his conflicting thoughts into a coherent explanation even if he wanted to. Frankie remained silent, sipping her own coffee and looking away from him.

Finally, he answered, "I'm thinking about Dad and wondering what I should do about him."

Frankie did look at him then, her eyes filled with understanding.

"Maybe I can help?" she offered. "I mean, I can't make the decision for you, but I've observed a lot of seniors and I've seen what their families go through. It might even help to just talk about it."

"It might," Ben conceded. But he stayed silent. While it was true that his thoughts were always edged with worry about his father, he was also trying to comprehend the mixture of traits—hard and defensive, soft and empathetic—that composed his summer neighbor.

Propelled by Ben's continued silence and the grim edginess around his eyes and mouth that spoke of weariness and concern, Frankie had the urge to share her goal with him, an offering of sorts. She would give a little and then, perhaps, he would find it easier to talk to her. It was strange, she pondered, how she had almost forgotten the rhythmic dance of give and take that could occur between friends…if that's what she and Ben were.

"When you saw me writing on the beach," she began slowly, "I was… I was writing down some things that I want to happen after this summer is over."

Although Ben's eyes lit with interest, he let her take her time and didn't prod.

Frankie appreciated that about him, and it occurred to her that she appreciated other things about him, as well, not the least of which was the way he treated Rae. He wasn't used to being around children, she knew, but he never talked down to Rae, as Rae's dad had been prone to do, and he took her feelings into consideration. Really, when she thought about it, after the brief misunderstanding when he'd first seen them at the cabin, Ben had been nothing but considerate to both of them.

And, if she occasionally caught herself admiring the dark blue in his eyes and the sun in his hair, there was no harm in that…was there?

Frankie realized that Ben was still waiting for her answer.

"I want to be a nurse," she said, savoring the words as she spoke them. The more she said them, the more right and true they felt. But when the words left her mouth and were out there for Ben to hear, she remembered her ex-husband's reaction and criticism and braced herself.

The touch on her hand was warm and soothing, penetrating through to some fragile and almost forgotten part of her. For a moment, Frankie closed her eyes and savored the reassurance in that touch, the comfort. She didn't even associate it with Ben or really register that he had pulled his chair closer to hers.

When she opened her eyes and saw him looking at her, she was embarrassed, though his eyes were filled with admiration.

"That's a fantastic goal," he said. "I honestly don't know anyone who I think would make a better nurse than you would."

"Well…thanks." Frankie tried to shrug away his enthusiasm. She didn't want to need it; she didn't want it to touch an emotional core within her the way it was.

But when she looked back at him again, the admiration remained. His hand on hers remained, warm and, somehow, full of promise.

She wanted to take it all in, to believe that she deserved it.

Suddenly Ben dropped her hand and bolted upright.

"Do you hear that?" he asked, already moving off the deck before Frankie could react.

She saw him headed at a hurried pace back toward his own cabin and followed him, guessing that he feared that Al had slipped out and would be on the run.

As Frankie reached the side of their cabin, she heard some loud rustling and grunts as if a physical struggle ensued. She darted quickly around to the back, in anticipation of helping Ben subdue his father.

To her shock, it wasn't Al that he struggled with. It was a thin teenage boy. His cutoff jeans were splattered with paint, and he thrashed and fought like a wild animal in Ben's unrelenting grip.

"He was about to decorate the back of our cabin," Ben said, his mouth in a grim, white line.

"In the middle of Sunday afternoon?" Frankie gasped inanely. Then she gathered herself enough to say, "I'll go get help."

"It's okay," Ben said. "I've got him. But if you could stay close by in case Dad wakes up?"

"Yes. Yes, of course. It might be best if I just sit over at your cabin, if you think Al won't be too startled at seeing me when he wakes up."

"He's startled seeing *me* when he wakes up," Ben said bluntly. He had one strong arm firmly around the boy's midriff.

"I have to get going," he said, his voice growing choppy with exertion. "Make yourself at home. I'll be back as soon as I can."

Frankie watched as Ben maneuvered the boy into the front seat of his car and she could see that, in the midst of everything, he was being very careful not to hurt him.

She popped quickly back to her own cabin to let Rae know where she would be, explaining only that Ben had something he had to do.

Rae lifted her head from her work. She had the look that Frankie thought of as being "fuzzy around the edges," when she pulled herself a long way from where her attention had been to where it needed to be. As always, there was a slight twinge in Frankie's heart when she saw her daughter with her lopsided glasses and her unfurling braids.

"Can I come, too?" Rae asked.

"If you want to," Frankie said. "Or would you rather keep working on your art here?" She studied the sketch that Rae had been working on—two beaver faces peeking out from their dam—and said, "This is very good. I'm so happy you are drawing again."

Rae shrugged but looked pleased.

"Anyway, you can stay here, or grab some things and come with me. They're both fine, but I can't wait too long in case Al wakes up."

Rae sprang into action, gathering up her picture and pencils.

At Ben's cabin, Frankie quickly checked on Al, who was still asleep. It was a relief for the time being, but she felt bad thinking what that would mean for Ben later on.

The events outside of the cabin had happened so quickly that she'd hardly had time to register them. As time passed and Ben still hadn't returned, anxiety began to overtake Frankie. For Rae's sake, she strove to keep a calm demeanor.

Thankfully, Rae was contentedly absorbed in her sketching.

What was taking Ben so long? What were his plans for the boy?

Something niggled in the back of Frankie's mind, telling her that maybe she should pray about it.

Before she could decide if she wanted to acknowledge that thought, Rae put her pencils aside with a deeply satisfied sigh and asked, "How much longer do we have to be here?"

"I'm not sure," Frankie answered. "I thought Ben would be back by now."

"Mom?"

"Yes?"

There was silence.

"Yes, what is it, Rae?"

Rae picked up one of her pencils again and,

tracing over a circle again and again, she asked, her eyes on the paper, "Are you going to marry Ben?"

Frankie still hadn't made sense of what it was she had felt on the deck before Ben caught the boy, and now wasn't the time to start. No doubt Rae was thinking back to what she had heard the ladies talking about at church, even though she—and Ben—had done their best to reassure Rae that it was just idle chitchat and didn't warrant her worry.

But the pencil stilled on the paper and she knew Rae was waiting for an answer.

"Ben and I are just friends," Frankie replied. "Acquaintances, really," she added for good measure. "I don't plan to get married again."

Rae raised her head slowly and looked at her mom with more questions in her eyes.

"Some moms and dads get married again to other people."

"Yes," Frankie agreed. "Some do. I don't intend to."

She held Rae's eyes until her daughter gave a brief nod, picked up her pencil and began to draw again.

Frankie was relieved that Rae was satisfied, but why then, she asked herself, did it suddenly hurt to give that answer? Was she going to have to spend the rest of her life judging men by

Trevor's behavior? Was that even fair to do, especially when someone like Ben continuously demonstrated to her that he was nothing like that?

The door to the cabin clicked open suddenly and she looked in its direction, anxious to hear what had happened.

She was surprised to see that Ben wasn't alone. The boy he had caught vandalizing was still with him.

## Chapter Eleven

When she saw the boy standing still and not fighting Ben, despite the colossal scowl on his face, Frankie realized just how young he really was. She didn't think he could be any older than fourteen and wasn't particularly large for his age, either. He was thin and his brown hair hung into his eyes the way some young people wore it these days.

Questions tangled in her head. Why had Ben brought him back here? What must Rae be thinking?

But Rae studied the stranger with curiosity and a dollop of shyness, and Frankie realized that in her daughter's eyes, this was just a teenage boy, not someone who had frightened an entire community.

Come to think of it, was it really possible that this scrawny boy with the darting eyes *was* the cause of all that? Frankie wondered now if the evidence was only circumstantial.

She had so many things she wanted to ask Ben.

Her eyes sought his to enquire what was going on. In the expression on his face, she read clearly, *Don't worry, I'll fill you in.*

Al took that moment to wake up, shouting out his groggy displeasure from his room. Ben went to attend to him, saying over his shoulder, "Keep an eye on him, will you?" He jerked his head toward the boy.

"But what if he…?" Frankie protested, trying not to sound as nervous about the situation as she felt.

"He's not going to run, are you, Danny?" Ben's words were soft, but they most definitely had pointed edges.

The boy didn't answer; instead, he remained where he was standing as if frozen to the spot. His shoulders and arms were tense at his sides.

"I'll be right back," Ben said.

There was silence, punctuated only by Rae's pencil making a soft, scratching sound on the paper.

After a few minutes, she lifted her head from her work and asked the boy, "Is Ben your dad?"

The boy jerked, almost a convulsive motion, and glared at Rae.

"No!" he said. Even his voice was younger than Frankie expected, cracked with adolescence. "What are you? Stupid?"

"Hey, watch it," Frankie warned him. He subsided but his eyes stabbed at her.

Ben returned with Al in tow and took stock of the scenario that awaited him:

Rae appeared wounded but dignified. Frankie stood in her familiar hands-on-hips stance, her face sporting a ferocious scowl, and Danny looked slightly shell-shocked.

Despite the severity of what had been thrown into his lap, Ben experienced a jolt of amusement. He guessed that Danny hadn't seen Frankie coming.

The brief, jovial moment passed when he saw that the boy was fixing him with a look filled with both fear and fury and that Frankie's expression so acutely demanded an explanation she might as well have hung a sign around her neck.

"You can't keep me here," Danny said. "I'll charge you with kidnapping or somethin'."

"Is that before or after we discuss your artistic endeavors?" Ben replied drily. "Besides, your grandma knows you're with me, so you might as well settle in. She'll come get you when she's ready. Do you want something to eat?"

Confusion reigned on Danny's face. Ben could tell that he couldn't piece together someone who was going to make sure he paid his dues with someone who would offer him food.

"No?" he said uncertainly.

Rae announced that she was going back to her own cabin. "I don't like him!" she declared haughtily.

Frankie nodded and murmured that she would be there as soon as she could and that Rae should come get her if she needed anything. Ben could see that she was distracted and troubled by a litany of unanswered questions.

Her mother lion ferocity had subsided and she once again appeared fragile and vulnerable, eyes shadowed with worry.

"You!" Ben's father roared, snatching back all the attention. Al was glaring at Danny. Was it possible he knew or had seen something that he hadn't been able to express? Then again, it could just be his father directing an outburst to the nearest target.

To his surprise, Danny didn't appear to be particularly rattled or concerned by the force of Al's negative attention.

"Me," he replied simply and didn't look away from Al's glare.

Al jabbed a finger in the air at him a few

times, then mumbled something and his emotions quieted down.

Well, that's interesting, Ben thought.

He saw that Frankie had noticed, too; her head tilted to one side, her eyes speculative. He couldn't put off talking to her any longer, Ben thought. He needed it as much as she did.

He got his dad settled with a bowl of cornflakes and directed Danny to sit at the table with him.

"We'll be right outside," he cautioned.

The boy made an ugly face but sat down without protest.

Once they were outside, Ben suggested that they move away from the cabin a bit so that Danny wouldn't overhear their conversation.

"You must be wondering what's going on," he said. He congratulated himself for making the understatement of the year.

He expected Frankie to point that out to him, but she only nodded and kept her anxious eyes fixed on him.

"Oh, boy," he said and scratched his head. "Where do I start with this?"

"How about at the beginning?" she suggested. "You got him in your car and…"

"Well, at first we just drove around. I couldn't get him to tell me anything, not his name— nothing."

Ben paused, took a breath and scaled his fingers through his hair, signaling the agitation he felt.

"Why didn't you just drive him to the police station?" Frankie demanded. "They do have one here, don't they?"

"There are local authorities, yes."

"So?"

Ben shrugged, feeling a bit like a scolded schoolboy.

"I'm not sure I can explain," he said finally. "He was just so much younger than I expected. I couldn't get my head around this skinny kid being the cause of all the fear and speculation."

"But you found out that he was?" Frankie asked. "I mean, for sure?"

"Yes," Ben said. "The strange thing is that once he got talking, he had quite a bit to say. It was almost like he had just been waiting for someone to tell his story to."

After a moment, Frankie nodded, and he could see in her eyes that she, too, had seen something in Danny that made her hesitate in seeking his punishment.

"Were you right?" she asked. "Does he have too much money and time?"

"It sounds like his parents do," Ben answered. "Danny has been left with his grandmother for the summer, apparently for them to hash out a divorce settlement."

"Oh, I see," Frankie said very quietly.

"Yes."

"Do you know his grandma?" Frankie asked. "Is she a regular in the community?"

"She might have looked a little familiar, but we didn't know each other by name until today."

"I take it she didn't know what her grandson has been doing?"

"She might have suspected," Ben said. "It's hard to say." He hesitated, wanting his words to be accurate but not cruel. "She strikes me as a woman who doesn't cope with things very well."

Frankie's face revealed that she struggled with the same mixed emotions that he did. He'd somehow had an unquestionable certainty that she would understand, the same way she understood the complex struggles he had with his father.

It didn't take a genius to realize that the boy was acting out deep emotional wounds. Still, there would be consequences for his actions.

"I still don't understand why he's back here with you," Frankie said.

"Danny's grandma knows that the authorities will have to deal with this," Ben answered. "She asked me if I would do her the favor of keeping

Danny with me for just another hour or so while she prepares herself. I felt badly for her—for both of them—so I said I would."

Distress brewed on Frankie's face. Ben knew she thought he had possibly put them in jeopardy.

Ben sighed. "I honestly did what I thought was best in that moment," he said. "I have to believe she's doing as much as she can. She's not a young woman anymore by any means, and I can't help thinking how all of this—" he made a sweeping gesture with his arm "—has been dumped on her without her wanting it. She says that Danny is a good boy at heart and I want to believe her."

He added silently, *Because the Lord knows we all do things we regret doing.*

Frankie looked thoughtful. "What do you think?" she asked. "I trust your opinion."

Surprise and gratitude blossomed in Ben at Frankie's declaration of trust, and he noted that she looked a bit surprised at her own words. She kept her eyes on his as she waited for his answer.

"I tend to agree with her," he said slowly.

"You think Danny is a good person?"

"I don't think he's a truly bad one," he clarified. "I…" He hesitated, not sure how much he should say. "I feel that on some level I understand him."

He could tell that Frankie was waiting for him to explain himself further, but he didn't want to get into all of that, not with his dad and Danny waiting inside.

"Even so," Frankie said, "something has to be done."

"Something will be done," Ben said. "It will be over with soon enough and we can get back to enjoying our summers. For right now, though," he said, "we'd better go back inside and make sure everything's okay. At least, I'd better."

Frankie opened her mouth as if she was about to say something, then clamped it shut.

"I should get back to Rae." She furrowed her brow. "I wonder what I should tell her."

"The truth," Ben suggested gently. "It seems to be working well so far. She's a very resilient person—like her mom."

That observation appeared to fluster her, but at the same time there was a spark of gratitude in her eyes.

After enlisting a promise that he would keep her posted, Frankie returned to her own cabin and at once Ben felt acutely alone. The last thing in the world he wanted to do was go back inside the cabin to deal with his postnap grumpy father and a surly teen with issues very likely deeper than he could contend with.

He cautiously opened the cabin door and tried not to envision some sort of wreckage or the severe agitation that Danny might provoke in his dad.

He was not at all prepared for the sight that met his eyes. His father and Danny sat side by side at the kitchen table, utterly engrossed in folding towels.

## Chapter Twelve

Frankie found Rae in her room, flipping through a book about animals that she had picked up from the library. Frankie knew her daughter was studying the finer details and poses of the animals for possible sketches later.

"I need to tell you something, Sweet Pea." Frankie sat on the end of the bed and said, "Danny—the boy that Ben brought back with him—well, he's the one who's been vandalizing around here. His parents are getting a divorce and he's very upset about it."

Rae sat still for what felt like a long time, her face in repose. Frankie watched her anxiously, but Rae looked thoughtful rather than upset.

"It's like he can't help it, like Al. Right, Mom?" she finally said.

"What do you mean?" Frankie asked.

"Well, like there's something sad and scared

in him that has to come out," Rae explained. "Al yells and sometimes says things that he shouldn't and Danny draws those bad pictures."

Wordlessly, Frankie reached for Rae and gathered her into a hug so tight that Rae eventually squirmed and said, "Ow! Mom!"

"I'm sorry," Frankie said, "but you are, like, the best kid ever."

"I still don't like Danny," Rae said, making sure that was very clear. "He called me stupid."

"Which everyone knows isn't true in the least," Frankie said. "Danny is a very unhappy person, and often people like that try to make sure that everyone around them feels the same way. It's up to us to make sure he doesn't succeed."

"How long will he be with Ben and Al?" Rae wondered. Her face puckered with worry. "He won't do anything to hurt them, will he?"

"I don't think so. I'm sure that Ben has things under control."

"We should go see," Rae declared. She put her book to the side and swung her legs around. "Let's go!"

Frankie had been hoping for a longer reprieve from the situation, but she felt she couldn't do that to Rae. She considered her daughter's perceptive reaction and thought again about what

Ben had said, about Rae being resilient—perhaps more so than she gave her credit for.

Rae *had* been a strong, unique little girl, before the whole situation with her ex-husband. And this time in Silver Lake was all about healing. But when they returned to Ben's cabin and saw his face lit with surprise at seeing her again so soon, and she thought about the support he had given her, she suddenly wondered if what she really wanted was more complex.

Ben rose from his chair and met them at the door. "Check this out," he said under his breath, and tilted his head in the direction of Al and Danny.

"How long do you think he'll be here?" Frankie hissed her question.

Rae folded her arms across her chest like a barrier and shifted from one foot to another.

"That's not the point," Ben said, his voice edging into impatience. "Look at what they're doing."

Frankie observed the unusual pair for a couple of minutes: Al would fold a towel, then would get agitated and shake it out with a violent jerk. Danny would patiently pick it up and smooth it out and hand it back to him.

She narrowed her eyes thoughtfully.

"They've been doing that since you left," Ben explained quietly. "He—Danny—won't give me the time of day, but he's sure been good with Dad."

"That's good," Frankie said slowly as her mind explored the implications. "I'm just surprised he's still here."

Ben checked his watch. "I should probably get him back," he agreed, "and check on his grandma."

Frankie saw his eyes cloud with worry as he confessed, "I kind of lost track of time and I was enjoying the peace and quiet."

"I get that," Frankie said.

She noticed that Rae had edged closer to the table where they sat and heard her daughter, in a small but resolute voice, say, "I'm not stupid." Then she added for good measure, "Al is *my* friend."

Ben raised his eyebrows at Frankie in a slightly comical look, and Frankie had to smile in return, noting how Rae had rallied herself to mark her territory. An instant later, her nerves were on high alert for how Danny would respond.

He tilted his head up in Rae's direction and Frankie assumed he was looking at her, though it was hard to tell under that concealing curtain of hair.

"I guess you should help then," he said, and tossed a handful of towels in her direction.

Frankie watched Rae bend over to retrieve them and her thoughts zigzagged in all directions. What kind of a person was Danny, really?

When she looked over at Ben, his face reflected her puzzlement.

The tap at the cabin door startled both of them.

*It's Danny's grandma*, Ben mouthed to Frankie as he opened the door.

"I know you said you'd bring Danny back," the older woman said. "But I thought I'd better take him off your hands even though I still have this headache…" She grimaced and touched two fingers delicately to her temple.

She had one of those whispery but wheedling voices, Frankie thought, as if she's used to making excuses.

*Help me not to be so judgmental.* Frankie caught herself up short. Had she just prayed?

"I'm Irma Conroy," she said, introducing herself to Frankie. Her hand felt cold and bony within Frankie's grasp.

Under the circumstances it hardly seemed appropriate to respond with *Nice to meet you*, so Frankie mustered a smile and said, "I guess there's a lot to think about."

"Daniel's parents will be here tomorrow to deal with the authorities." Irma winced as if the words caused her physical pain.

Frankie felt an acute stab of sympathy for the boy. She knew that what he had done wasn't right and that there had to be consequences, but he was so young—not much older than Rae—and there were clearly extenuating circumstances in his life. Not that she should be making excuses for him, but still…

She saw Ben looking at the boy, and his face mirrored her own conflicting feelings.

He said quietly, "I hope that they can work out something that benefits everyone, including Danny."

"Well, we shall see," Irma said. "It's out of my hands."

She told Danny that it was time to go. Just as they were about to make their exit, Frankie blurted out, "How is he so good with Al? I mean, how does he know…?"

Irma looked slightly taken aback at the question.

"Oh," she said. "His grandfather had horrible dementia before he passed on. Daniel always had a lot of patience with him."

"Was that your husband?" Ben asked.

"Yes. It was a dreadful time."

"I'm sure it was," Ben said. After a moment he added, "I will pray for you and your family. I'll pray that God helps all of you with the decisions you'll have to make."

Irma hesitated for a moment, then gave a brief nod.

"Thank you," she said. "Come, Daniel. Please thank Ben and his wife again for their hospitality."

Frankie's mouth flew open to correct the misconception, but they were gone before she could.

The shock of those words felt like a slap, like a joke at which she had no desire to laugh.

Then she noticed Ben's mouth quirking in that familiar way.

"What?" she demanded.

"Nothing—it's just that you don't have to look quite so appalled at the thought of being married to me."

Frankie could see Rae at the table, pretending not to listen. Her cheeks were red and her hands had paused over the pile of towels. Frankie decided that she'd better quickly change the subject.

"What do you think they'll do to him?" she asked. "I'm still hoping for community service."

"I'm trying to trust that God has a good plan for Danny's life," Ben said. "Sit down, if you like. I'll make coffee or there's tea or juice if you want."

"Tea would be nice," Frankie said. "Whatever you choose is good."

Settled into one of those old couches with a flowered pattern that Frankie was sure must grace every cottage in Canada, her thoughts returned to Irma's words.

It shouldn't rattle her so much, she thought. It was an innocent mistake. But she wasn't a wife anymore. She roused herself from those hurtful musings when Ben handed her a cup of tea. But when she took it from him and the tips of their fingers touched briefly, she considered that perhaps those feelings weren't as dead as she thought they were.

"Quite the day," he said.

She took a sip and nodded. "Was it really just this morning that we were at church?"

"Yup, hard to believe." Ben took a sip from his own cup. "Is this okay? Too strong?"

"It's fine, thank you."

They sat in silence, each lost in thought. At the table, Al and Rae put the towels aside and Al watched, with some pointing and blurted suggestions, as Rae worked on a puzzle.

"Did you eat again?" Ben asked. "I think we should have something."

*We*, Frankie thought. It was such an easy word to say but so hard to be part of. But Ben disarmed her in ways she hadn't anticipated and she didn't know how she felt about that.

Her speculations were taken over by hunger

pangs. "I guess I am hungry," she said. "I didn't even realize until now. Rae, you must be hungry, too."

"I had a banana," Rae said calmly, her eyes on the puzzle.

"Dad's usually not too subtle about letting me know when he's hungry," Ben admitted. "Still, I should probably get something started because you never know when that will happen. Would you like to join us? Please?" He looked pointedly in the direction of his absorbed father, and Frankie understood.

"What can I bring over?" she asked. She admitted to herself that after the events of the day, she wasn't exactly in the mood for a meal with just her and Rae.

"Anything is fine, whatever you have. If you want to bring things to make a salad, that would be great."

Frankie returned briefly to her own cabin to rustle up salad ingredients and managed to find some lettuce, a few carrots and a lone tomato. It wasn't bad, but if Ben had things in his refrigerator they could combine ingredients and make it even better.

As Ben made hamburger patties to put on the grill, his mind went back over the day. He tried to convince himself not to get too invested in the decision about Danny, because ultimately he had no say. But there was definitely something about the boy he could relate to. Besides that, his thoughts kept returning to Frankie. He couldn't make head nor tail of her sometimes. She was the most contradictory and stubborn woman he had ever met…and the most intriguing.

She appeared out of her cabin then, juggling an assortment of items. He saw her face, a study in concentration as she made her way down the rickety steps, and it made him smile.

"I didn't have as much in the fridge as I thought," she said apologetically as she deposited her contribution on the table. "I could run to the store."

"You don't have to," Ben said. "Thanks for bringing this. I can probably find a few things to add."

"That's what I was hoping," Frankie said.

"Besides, if we do need something from the store, it gives me something to do if Dad gets restless and wants to go for a walk."

"Those two have been at it a long time," Frankie observed.

"Yes," Ben agreed. "Dad is having a pretty good day. I like to think that it's God's way of giving me a bit of a reprieve. I mean, not having to deal with the whole Danny issue and with Dad having a bad day at the same time."

When the words were out of his mouth, Ben expected Frankie to retort something along the lines that if God really wanted to give him a reprieve, He wouldn't have given him *any* of it to deal with.

To his surprise, though, she was quiet, thoughtful.

He was even more surprised when she blurted out, "I think I prayed today."

"You're not sure?" Then he realized he didn't want her to think that he doubted her or that he was making light of her statement, so he added quickly, "That's good— that's great!"

Frankie chewed her lip and pondered. "I asked for something," she said. "It was just very quick and spur-of-the-moment, but it felt like—I don't know—it felt like I was talking to someone, and not just thinking the thought. Do you know what I mean? At least it felt like I wanted to talk to someone."

"That's really good," Ben said again.

*Lord, thank You for reminding me that You're still at work in people's lives.*

"What do you think it means?" Frankie asked him.

"I think only you can decide what it means to you," Ben said, choosing his words carefully, praying silently as he did so. "But it could mean that you're ready to consider a relationship with God again."

Frankie narrowed her eyes.

"I know He's there," she said. "I just didn't think He'd done anything to help us, after, well…" Her voice trailed off.

"And what do you think now?" Ben asked.

She studied his face as if the answer was somehow written there.

"I think," she said, "that I still have a lot of thinking to do."

A disgruntled sound came from Al. "Hurry!" he demanded, pointing at the hamburger patties.

"And it hits," Ben murmured. He transferred the patties onto a plate and carried them to the grill.

"Come on, Dad," he said. "You can supervise."

"Okay," Al said agreeably.

"Rae and I will make the salad," Frankie said. "Rae, please clean up the table and come help me."

Ben saw Rae's face crinkle in mild rebellion, but she obeyed her mother, put the puzzle back in its box and gathered up the towels.

On his way outside, Al stopped and pointed his finger at Frankie.

"Wife!"

Ben saw Frankie stiffen and saw the darting-eyed look that Rae gave her.

"Wife!" Al said again, and chortled loudly.

# *Chapter Thirteen*

Ben hurried his father outside, giving Frankie an apologetic look as he did so. Frankie believed that Al couldn't help what came blurting out of him, but honestly, being called Ben's wife twice in one day was a bit much.

Rae ran water over the lettuce in the sink.

"Do we have to eat here?" she whispered.

"Not if you really don't want to," Frankie said. "But I thought you and Al were having fun?"

Rae shrugged. "Can you please get me some paper towel?"

Frankie tore off a few pieces, handed them to her and waited.

Rae dabbed the towel at the lettuce leaves, soaking up their moisture. Keeping her eyes on what she was doing, she said, "Why did Danny's grandma call you Ben's wife?"

Frankie gently eased the paper towel out of her daughter's hands and put her hands on Rae's shoulders to guide her gaze.

When she was sure she had Rae focused on her she said, "Do you know what an assumption is?"

"Is that like a mistake?"

"In some cases, yes," Frankie explained. "When Danny's grandma assumed that I was Ben's wife, that was a mistake. And I know that you understand about Al, that he doesn't always know what he's saying."

"It's a mistake because you're Daddy's wife, right?" Rae asked with a watchful look.

"Not anymore, Sweet Pea," Frankie said, fighting to keep her tone even. "When people get divorced, they're not husband and wife anymore. We've talked about this."

Her daughter folded her arms and Frankie recognized her own stubborn look in the set of Rae's jaw.

"I don't *want* you to marry Ben," she declared emphatically.

"I have no intentions of marrying Ben," Frankie said. "Or anyone else."

Her wish to comfort and reassure Rae grappled with a feeling of resentment that was small but definitely there, enough so that guilt was nibbling at her heels again.

She didn't want to resent her own child, and she really didn't have any intentions of getting married again. But she couldn't help feeling that it might be nice if Rae hadn't so adamantly put her foot down about it.

Still, Rae was her daughter and her main concern and focus in life. She had to be patient with her and realize that she had as many complexities as the next person, regardless of age: she could be mature and perceptive when it came to things like her art and Al and even Danny, whom she scarcely knew. And if she regressed to childishness when she felt threatened by potential upheaval in her world, Frankie couldn't blame her.

"We can eat back at our place if you really want to," Frankie offered. "I'll tell Ben and I'm sure he'll understand."

"Are you going to tell him I said not to marry him?" Rae asked anxiously.

Frankie felt her mouth quirk, mimicking the expression she could picture on Ben's face, so she relinquished a bit to the humor in the situation.

"I think it would scare Ben just a little if I even mentioned marriage," she said. "I can say we had a change of plans."

Rae wrinkled her forehead, thinking. "But wouldn't that be impolite?" she finally asked.

"Well, I guess it might be."

"Remember when we were going to have company?" Rae continued. "And you worked really hard cooking for them, and at the last minute they said they had other plans and you said that—"

"Yes," Frankie cut her off, not eager to relive one of her less fine moments. Honestly, did her daughter have to remember everything?

"Now I'm confused," she said to Rae. "What do you want to do?"

"I guess we can stay," Rae conceded. "But don't sit beside Ben and don't do anything disgusting."

"Disgusting?"

"Like kiss him or something." Rae wrinkled her face up like she'd swallowed a worm.

"Once again," Frankie said solemnly, "I don't think that's going to be an issue."

Outside, Rae made a beeline for Al and sat in the chair beside him. Al showed her his sea-shell collection, which he had brought outside in a little plastic bag, and Rae murmured and exclaimed over them as if seeing them for the first time.

"That lettuce must have really needed washing," Ben said quietly to Frankie as she handed him the salad.

Her eyebrows arched a wary question.

He lowered his voice even more. "I promise not to do anything disgusting."

"You could hear?" Frankie was glad that the evening dusk hid her blush.

"Pretty much." Ben jerked his head toward the open kitchen window. "I know this will amaze you given how deluxe these cabins are, but they're not exactly soundproof."

Frankie was embarrassed; then she shrugged and answered his grin with one of her own.

Ben gave a long whistle. "Boy, oh boy," he said. "I sure feel sorry for them."

"For who? What are you talking about?"

"Those people that didn't show up for your dinner that night."

Ben's grin widened, and Frankie thought he looked more pleased with himself than he had any right to. He started to whistle again and sauntered off to check on the burgers.

Frankie watched him flip burgers with finesse and thought that he looked better than was good for her.

In that moment, Ben felt he'd never been more grateful that God had blessed him with a sense of humor. More than once it had helped alleviate awkward or even potentially painful situations. This one, he thought, had the ingredients to be both.

He'd never been married, let alone remarried, but he knew enough to understand that Rae's reactions were pretty much par for the course, so he wasn't taking it personally. It wasn't that he even had time to think about something like that, not with the continued care of his father. But when he'd gone to wake Al up from his nap earlier, he had noticed something that had somehow escaped him as he watched the disease devour his father's mind—the growing physical frailty of his father—and he couldn't help for a moment appreciating the thought of having someone he could share his worries and regrets with. And since Frankie already understood so much, it was understandable that she would come to mind.

The sky had darkened by the time they were finished with supper, and they watched a glorious sunset splash its crimson and coral colors.

"Who could look at that and think there wasn't a creator?" Ben asked. Then he was concerned that Frankie might think he was pushing his faith at her, and he darted a quick look her way.

But she studied the sky with a pensive expression as if she, too, was considering the implications of the cosmic work of art.

"Mom?" Rae's small voice piped into the silence. Ben watched Frankie stir and blink, a slow catlike blink, as if her thoughts had carried her somewhere far away.

"Yes, Rae?"

"Can Al and I walk down the road and back? We'll stay where you can see us."

"I think you'd better ask Ben," Frankie suggested.

Rae glanced over at him and then at her feet.

"Sure, you and Dad can go for a walk," Ben said, not making her ask him.

He and Frankie watched the little girl take Al's hand and carefully guide him around a stump near the path.

"Sorry about that," Frankie said. "She's feeling a bit threatened by our relation…" She let her voice trail off and Ben perceived that she didn't want to use a word with as much import as *relationship*.

"That's okay," he said.

Generally Ben considered himself a good-natured person, but even God's handiwork wasn't enough to keep his current melancholy thoughts at bay. For some reason tonight, the idea of so many unspoken words was bringing him down. He wished he could be sure that he had let his father know how much he had learned from him about God and people and life and that he was sorry for his mistakes. He wished that just one more time he could hear his dad say that everything was going to be all right.

He wished he could tell Frankie how beautiful she looked against the backdrop of the setting sun.

Instead, he chose to keep the conversation on their common ground, a place where they always met in understanding.

"I'm glad those two are okay," he said, indicating Al and Rae, who were making their way slowly along the path. "I mean, I'm glad Rae is okay with him. I still feel badly about what happened earlier."

Frankie turned her attention away from the sky.

"Not your fault," she said.

"Yes—well, it's hard not to feel responsible."

Silence brewed between them again. It wasn't an uncomfortable silence—Ben couldn't quite put his finger on what the feeling was—but the air itself seemed to pulsate with unspoken words.

"So," Ben said, causing her to start a little bit—not so much a jump as to show a physical awareness of his voice. "What did you end up telling Rae about Danny?"

"The truth," Frankie said. She studied her thumbnail as if it compelled her. "Like you suggested," she added.

"And she was okay with it?"

"She was surprisingly mature about it. I guess I shouldn't say *surprisingly*. Rae does have her eyes open to many things."

The regret in her voice told Ben that she wished that wasn't always the case.

"This holiday hasn't been what you've wanted it to be, has it?" he asked with compassion.

"No," Frankie admitted, "it hasn't. Maybe things will start to get better now. I mean, at least we have an answer about the vandalism. Anyway, it hasn't been all bad. The lake is beautiful and Rae loves her art classes."

"What have you found here to make you happy?"

"Me?" Frankie said. The question seemed to fluster her. "I—I guess I'm not much of one to sit around on the beach. I do like the lake, but I can't make myself stay there for hours at a time and it's not that much fun for me to browse in shops where I don't have a hope of buying anything."

"So, what have you found that you enjoy here?" Ben reiterated, hoping for one brief, foolish moment that she would say *you*.

She shrugged and he thought he saw a fleeting shadow of sadness pass over her face. It was quickly replaced by a determined smile.

"I guess that I'm just learning to be grateful

day by day. I've already come a lot further than I ever thought I would."

"I think that's wonderful," Ben said. "It isn't easy to move past things. Trust me, I know. There are so many things that I wish I could have the chance to do over."

He could see the questions on Frankie's readable face.

"I can't imagine you being anything but the perfect son," she said.

He studied his hands, noting calluses from all the work he'd done in his life. After a pause, he answered quietly, "I guess you need to work on your imagination then."

She didn't say anything, but he could tell by the stillness in the air between them that she was waiting for him to tell her more.

Something surged in his heart, revealing that he wanted to.

"I mentioned my mom had ovarian cancer and passed away?"

Frankie nodded and softly put her hand over his, her eyes radiating sympathy.

"Well," Ben continued, tasting regret as he said the words. "What I didn't tell you was that I didn't even come home. I didn't help Dad with anything and I wasn't there when she died."

He waited for Frankie's look of shock or disapproval, for her to recoil from the truth of the selfish person he was. But her hand remained where it was, and she waited for him to continue.

"I was doing missionary work," he said. "Being the good guy..." He heard the sarcastic tang in his own voice. "I think what I was really doing, though, was avoiding Dad and what I thought everyone expected of me, all the pressure I thought came with being his son. So, I'm not the perfect son." He chuckled mirthlessly. "Far from it."

"But you did truly accomplish valuable things through your missionary work," Frankie reminded him. "Whatever your motives were to start with. Anyone can see that you have genuine faith and that you love your father very much. I..." Her voice grew shy and hesitant. "I think you're a good man, Ben."

He closed his eyes, basking in the balm of the words and the warmth of her hand on his. When he opened his eyes, Frankie was looking at him as if she was contemplating something. Where he had expected judgment and rejection, she was showing acceptance and even affection. His gaze fell to her slightly parted lips and he felt himself slowly drawn toward them. Their lips touched gently. She didn't pull away.

His cell phone rang, shattering the fragile moment between them.

Frankie jumped back, looking disconcerted, like she had woken up from a puzzling dream. She touched her lips with the tips of her fingers.

Ben grabbed his phone and looked at it.

"It's Danny's grandmother," he said.

## Chapter Fourteen

If Frankie could find anything to be glad about in that moment, it was that Ben had stepped away to take the call and she was left alone to gather herself.

What kind of person was she? She had just barely finished reassuring Rae that she had nothing to worry about as far as she and Ben were concerned, and the next thing she knew, Ben was kissing her and she was letting him. Not only letting him but *enjoying* it.

To make matters worse, her anger at herself was forced to compete with the memories of the kiss. She could still see Ben looking at her like she was actually someone worth looking at, and she could smell his masculine pine-and-wind scent.

"Rae!" she called. She could hear the strain

in her own voice and she paused to calm herself before calling again.

"Rae, it's dark out now. I think you and Al better come back."

Rae and Al slowly made their way back, and Frankie was grateful for the darkness that hid the flush on her cheeks and the emotions in her eyes.

"Dark," Al observed, and then he began to fuss for his bedtime snack.

Ben glanced over and, from his increased head nodding and gestures, Frankie could see that he was anxious to wrap up the call.

"That was Danny's grandmother," he said again, when he returned to them. "Danny's parents are supposed to come out here tomorrow and they will deal with the authorities. She just thought we should know."

Frankie avoided looking at him. "Okay," she mumbled, busying her fingers with the tangles in Rae's hair.

She could feel Ben watching her as she continued to smooth Rae's hair.

Al's demands threatened to escalate and Frankie used the opportunity to excuse her and Rae.

"Thank you for sharing your supper," she said rather formally. "I think I'd better get this young miss home."

"Thank you again for bringing the salad," Ben replied in a tone Frankie couldn't quite decipher.

He led Al into the cabin, assuring him that he could have toast with peanut butter and bananas.

In their cabin, Frankie adjusted the water for Rae in the temperamental shower, and then she made herself a cup of peppermint tea and tried to focus on a nursing brochure she had picked up at the library. But that only reminded her of Ben's encouraging words.

Had she become so pathetic that she was ready to fling herself into the arms of the first man to be kind to her? Frankie didn't want to believe that about herself. She wanted to be strong and not need anyone, but she didn't know what to think anymore.

The next morning, after a fitful sleep, Frankie woke up and was relieved to note that the first person on her mind wasn't Ben, but Danny.

A strong conviction that she couldn't just ignore his situation nagged at her. It was true that she had no real reason to get involved, but her mother's heart couldn't help hoping that Danny would get a chance to redeem himself and enjoy life the way a boy his age should be able to.

*Is that right?* She wondered if she was praying. *Am I supposed to get involved?*

She thought that the best-case scenario would

be for Danny to be assigned to community service. A picture of him folding towels with Al flashed into her mind and an idea began to take root. Besides being genuinely concerned about Danny, she acknowledged that it was good to have something else to think about and shove her other clamoring emotions into the background.

Rae gobbled down her breakfast with a faraway look that meant she was already making sketches in her mind.

"Slow down," Frankie cautioned her. "You don't want to choke."

"I'm full," Rae announced immediately, and shoved her plate away.

"Okay then, missy, but you won't get to eat again for at least a couple of hours."

"Doesn't matter," Rae mumbled, gathering her art supplies.

Frankie sighed and smiled at the same time, knowing it was true. The creation of art would keep her daughter as *full* as she wanted to be, as it fed a different kind of hunger.

"Okay, same deal as always," Frankie said. "I'll be at the library at noon when you come out."

"What are you going to do today?" Rae asked, slowing down for the first time since she'd gotten out of bed and putting her full focus on her mom. "Will we find out what's going to happen to Danny?"

"Danny's parents will be here some time today, and they'll have to talk to the authorities and come up with the best way to deal with things."

Rae contemplated as she inhaled her lower lip in and out.

"Will Danny have to go to jail?" she asked.

"They don't put boys Danny's age in jail," Frankie explained. "The worst-case scenario is that he'll be put in a juvenile-detention facility, but even that would be extreme. I think most likely he'll get community service."

Rae nodded her head slowly. "That way he gets to do some good and maybe feel better about himself, right, Mom?"

Frankie hugged her. "You're one smart and awesome kid."

"Mom, you're squishing my sketches! Stop!"

After leaving Rae at the library, Frankie made her way back to the cabins.

When she spotted Ben, he was down on his hands and knees attempting to tie his dad's shoes. Al wouldn't keep his feet still, and he wore the poke-tongued look that made Frankie wonder, if only fleetingly, whether he knew when he was giving someone a bad time.

"Oh, hi." Ben sounded breathless as he angled his head up to see her. From the look on his face, Frankie knew that he was as anxious as she was—if not more so—to clear the air.

Contrarily, her mood shifted and she thought he didn't have to look so anxious to reassure her that the kiss had meant nothing. *Men!* Frankie thought with exasperation. One of these days she would remember the lesson that you couldn't trust them.

Then she observed the deep weariness beaded across Ben's face, and she knew that he couldn't help having other things on his mind.

"Are you and Al getting ready to go somewhere?" she asked.

"There's a care facility in town that can take Dad for a couple of hours," Ben explained. "I don't like to make a habit of it, but there are some days I really need to focus on other things. The trick is convincing Dad that it's a good idea to go." With a quick maneuver of his hands, while Al was distracted by their conversation, he double knotted both sets of shoelaces and stood up.

His own hair hadn't been combed, Frankie noticed, and his face had whisker stubble.

"Are you okay?" she asked, even as she thought it wasn't an entirely unattractive look on him.

Ben nodded. "Yes, I'm fine. I didn't sleep

very well last night, but that's becoming par
for the course. It's not just because of Dad this
time, though. I keep thinking about Danny and
what's going to happen and the impact on the
whole community."

"I know," Frankie said. "I mean, I know I
don't have the history with this place that you
do, but I can't get Danny out of my mind, either. He's so *young*."

Ben raked his fingers through his hair and
said, "As if I need more to worry about right
now." He looked off into the distance. "I wonder sometimes if this whole summer was a bad
idea. You know how they say God never gives
you more than you can handle? Well, sometimes
I wonder if He gives me a lot more credit than
He should."

"Don't think that way," Frankie urged. "It was
a wonderful idea to bring your dad here where
you shared so many memories. No one could
have anticipated the vandalism, and at least now
we have an answer to that. Everything will work
out, I'm sure of it. I can go with you to drop your
dad off, if you like."

Ben studied her for a moment. A light of affection seemed to glow softly in his eyes. "That
would be nice," he said.

Together they urged Al into the car. Ben
stopped to buy his dad a vanilla ice-cream cone

in the hopes that the treat would put him into an agreeable mood.

About half an hour later, they had dropped Al off at the care center and it had not been a pretty picture. Still, Ben seemed to breathe a little easier once they were on their way again.

After Al was dropped off, Frankie got into the front seat.

"Well, here we are again," Ben said as he started the car. He slid his gaze over her way and something in it told Frankie that he hadn't forgotten last night—he hadn't forgotten at all.

The challenges that his father posed and his concerns about the consequences for Danny and the town of the vandalism were not enough of a deterrent to keep Ben from thinking about the fact that he and Frankie had kissed.

He still couldn't decide if he was disappointed or relieved that his phone had rung when it did.

And now Frankie sat beside him, with her window down so that her hair, the color of autumn leaves in sunlight, was lifted gently by the breeze and blown about. She was close enough that he could smell her warm vanilla scent. He was grateful for her presence and realized how easily he could grow to count on it—to like having her there beside him.

*Please, Lord, I can't want that. I don't have*

*enough to give. Help me keep my focus where it needs to be.*

"I think I need to stop by Irma's," Ben said, breaking the silence. "I think she's a weak person but not a bad one, and she probably feels she's dealing with this on her own. And if Danny's parents have arrived, I want to meet them and talk about a few things." He chuckled without much mirth. "I kept telling the Lord that I had enough on my plate, but He wouldn't let me sleep until I agreed to do it."

Frankie gave one firm nod. "I'll go with you."

"You don't have to do that."

"I know I don't have to, but I'm doing it."

Irma's cottage was the type that had always made Ben feel on edge, like he had to be careful to slip his shoes off at the door and not touch anything with sandy fingers.

As they walked up the long, winding driveway, they could see someone looking out.

"They must have heard the car," Ben remarked.

Then the door flew open and Irma hurried toward them, wringing her hands.

"Thank goodness you're here!" she gasped. "All they've done since they arrived is fight!"

## Chapter Fifteen

"I don't know what prompted you to come, but I'm glad you did," Irma said as she ushered them into a large foyer painted in cool shades of light blue and mint green. "Their behavior isn't helping poor Daniel and when *he's* not arguing with her, he's on the phone with his lawyer."

"By 'he' I assume you mean Danny's father?" Ben asked.

Irma's face clearly showed her disdain as she replied, "Yes, the man that my daughter used to call her husband."

They were ushered into a formal-looking sitting room, and Ben thought of his childhoods at the lake and the way he'd been able to dash in and out of the cabin with his swim trunks on, trailing sand and water with him.

He was very sure that Danny wouldn't be allowed to do any such thing here.

Ben introduced himself and Frankie to Danny's parents, explaining that he had a neighborly concern.

"Colin Latimer," the man said tersely, only shaking Ben's extended hand for a split second. "And my wife—soon to be ex—Marie."

Colin wore a conspicuously expensive suit and had eyes that didn't land anywhere for long.

Danny's mother, Marie, was extremely thin, exquisitely dressed and obviously knew the right hairstyle and makeup to wear. But, Ben thought, she couldn't hold a candle to Frankie, who was dressed in a simple red sundress and had pulled her hair back into a loose bun. Once again his growing fondness and admiration of Frankie surged through him.

But he had to focus on the reason for their visit.

Ben spotted Danny slouched in a low-slung chair near the entryway to a very large kitchen.

"Is it okay if we all sit down for a moment?" he asked.

Irma jumped slightly, as if startled out of her own thoughts. "Please," she said, gesturing to the chairs.

They all took seats. Irma and Marie mimicked each other's sighs and pressed their fingers to their temples.

"So why are you here?" Colin asked.

"To offer support as summer neighbors," Ben said. "To say I hope things work out well for Danny and that you all get through this. What time is court?"

"One o'clock," Colin said.

"I'll pray for you then," Ben offered.

Colin made a slight noise that made plain his opinion of prayer. "Well, thank you for your concern," he said in a tone that belied his words. "I'm sure we'll figure out the best way to deal with Danny, one way or another."

Frankie's eyes signaled to Ben exactly what she thought of the man's attitude. "Colin," Marie protested feebly. "I'm sure these nice people mean well."

"Oh, be quiet, Marie," Colin said with great exasperation.

"Really, Colin," Irma shrilled. "Have some respect. You don't hear Ben speaking that way to his wife."

Ben opened his mouth to explain that Frankie wasn't his wife, but Frankie caught his eye and shook her head as if to say there was no point complicating matters more than they already were.

If he was ever lucky enough to have a wife like Frankie, he thought, he would never in a million years talk to her that way.

"We certainly don't mean to overstep any

boundaries," Ben said, keeping his tone mild with some effort. "If there's anything we can do to make this situation easier…"

Despite the circumstances and unpleasant atmosphere, something chimed in his mind about how nice it felt to say *we*.

"We'll be sure to let you know," Colin said. His phone beeped, and he pulled it out of his pocket and studied it, frowning. "I guess that's it, then?" he said, stabbing at the keyboard.

Ben stood up and Frankie followed suit.

"Will you let me know how it goes?" Ben directed his question to Irma, who nodded and then stood up to walk them to the door."

"I'd appreciate the prayers," she said quietly, as she showed them out. "Thank you for thinking of us."

"I really appreciated having you with me, Frankie," Ben said, as they drove over to pick up his father.

"You're welcome," Frankie said. She took a deep, calming breath. She wasn't sure what had rattled her more: the tension in the atmosphere at Irma's cottage or yet another assumption that she and Ben were in a relationship.

Yet her mind didn't push the thought away as urgently as it would have before. Ben was a good, solid man and he cared about others. Even though he already had considerable responsibilities to deal with, he had taken the time to offer assistance and she admired him for that.

Maybe, she mused, it was time to stop assuming that there were no decent men in the world just because of the actions of men like Trevor—and Danny's father.

"Could Danny's parents make it any more obvious that they're wrapped up in their own problems?" Ben said grimly. "I truly do pray that things go well for the poor kid."

"Me, too," Frankie said very softly.

Ben glanced her way, his eyebrows raised in a question. Then he smiled warmly.

"Remember how good Danny was with your dad?" she asked.

"Yes."

"Well, I don't have it all thought out yet, but what if there was some way that Danny could pay his dues to the community by helping you with Al?"

"Like the youth-senior partnership program you told me about where you work?"

"Something like that, yes."

Ben nodded slowly. "I think it has potential," he said. "We'll have to hear from Irma what the judge has to say. I was also thinking that I could put him to work with a hammer and some paint." His mouth twitched and he added, "Paint used in the right way, of course."

Frankie couldn't help her snort of laughter, which caused Ben to laugh, too.

After a moment she sobered again and said, "I want you to know that I think it was very good of you to do what you did today."

"Not that it did much good," Ben said. "Colin made me feel a bit like I was a bug that had got into his salad and he was wondering the quickest way to get rid of me."

"Well…still, you tried to do something and that was more than many people would have done. It was certainly more than… It was way more than my ex would have done."

Ben's gaze slid over her way and Frankie could see curiosity softened by caring in his eyes.

She watched her hands on her lap, clenching and unclenching.

"He left me," she said, not looking up. "He said I hadn't met his expectations." She swallowed and cleared her throat. "In any way whatsoever."

Ben didn't say anything, but he reached out and took her hand, enveloping it in his large, warm one.

"I didn't know your ex-husband," he said finally. "But I can tell you one thing about him. He was wrong—completely and utterly wrong.

You're a remarkable woman, Frankie, and I don't want you to ever forget that."

Frankie took another deep breath. "Thank you," she said. "Thank you for saying that."

She'd try her best to believe it, she thought.

But she had told Ben something that she hadn't said out loud to another person, not in the words that captured the harsh depths of the betrayal. She had said the words out loud and they hadn't destroyed her, or made him think less of her.

She realized suddenly how much it meant to her that Ben Cedar not think less of her.

"Are you good for time?" Ben asked, as they headed toward the nursing home. "Or should I drop you off at the library before I get Dad?"

Frankie checked the time on the dashboard. "I'm good," she said, and Ben cast a smile of appreciation her way, warming her from head to toe. She felt that everything was going to turn out okay.

That feeling was almost instantly shattered when they stepped inside the nursing home. The coordinator swept down on Ben and said, in an almost accusing tone, "Thank goodness you're back on time. Your father was extremely difficult."

Frankie watched the shadow of deep, gripping weariness creep over Ben's face again, and she felt bad for him. He hadn't even had time to recuperate from one tense situation before being thrown directly into another.

"I'm sorry to hear that," Ben said. "What was the problem?"

"Pretty much everything," replied a woman named Eunice as she hustled them through to her office for Ben to sign papers that indicated he'd picked his father up.

"He refused to sit down for the group activity," she said. "He was belligerent with one of the volunteers. It upset her so much, in fact, that she had to go cry in the staff room. And he shoved one of the other participants."

With each declaration, Frankie watched Ben's head droop lower, as if the words were like sharp stones being pelted at his head.

She wanted to take his hand and offer him comfort and support. Reassure him that it wasn't his fault.

He raised his head then. "What do you suggest I do, Eunice?" he asked in a voice thick with defeat.

Eunice softened. "Oh, Ben," she said. "I know you and I know your father, and I know what kind of man he was. I see the things that this wicked disease can do to people, and I feel for you. But my job here is to protect everyone, and I can't have that kind of behavior going on. You understand that, don't you?"

"Yes," Ben said, "I understand, but that doesn't necessarily help."

"I think it's time to think about full-time care, don't you?" Eunice prodded. "It's really the best thing for Al, and for you."

A challenge flared in Ben's eyes. "How can I even think about putting him in full-time care when he's miserable for just a morning?" he demanded.

Eunice acknowledged his frustration. "It's one of the sad ironies of the disease that the more they need the care, the more they will rebel against it. It's not easy, I know, but I also know it's only going to get harder from here on out."

Ben studied his hands and Frankie noticed that the slight tremble in them matched the one in her own.

*Please, God, help him get through it and to make the right decision.* It occurred to her that it felt natural and right to pray for Ben, and for his father.

"I know I have a lot to think about," Ben said. "I'll pray about it."

"Okay then," Eunice said, "I'll take you to get your father. Now, Ben," she cautioned, "I don't want you to be upset when you see him. I want you to understand that we did everything we could before we resorted to putting him in the restraint chair."

"The restraint chair?" Ben repeated, and the crack in his voice sent an answering fissure through Frankie's heart.

She knew the chairs were a necessary evil in some circumstances, but couldn't help wondering if, for the few hours Al was there, they could have managed without it. She could tell by the stormy look on Ben's face that he was thinking the same thing.

Although she had seen the chairs used before, as long as she lived, Frankie didn't think she'd forget the disturbing sight of Al slumped in the chair with the belt strapped around his waist, and his face folded in defeat.

But even more heart-wrenching than that was the look on Ben's face when he saw his father in such a position.

"I don't understand it," he kept saying as he got Al into the car. "I don't understand. It's barely been two months. You saw him at the beginning of the summer. He asked Rae to play with him. How could he need to be strapped up like that? I don't understand."

Frankie knew that he wasn't truly asking her for an answer. She put her hand on his arm gently and looked at him until he returned her gaze.

"After I get Rae, we'll talk about this," she promised. "You won't have to make this decision alone. I'm here for you, and I'll pray for you."

Ben's eyes were cloudy with despair as they focused on hers, and then something subtly altered in his expression.

"Did you say you'd pray for me?" he asked.

Frankie nodded. "I guess," she said, "that thinking about some of the things you've said has helped me realize that God has been with us.

"I mean," she added hastily, "I still have to sort some things out and I'm still not thrilled with what Rae and I have gone through. But I'm learning to see His hand in what we do have and how He's brought us through."

"I'm very glad to hear that," Ben said, "and I'm very glad you're here."

Almost before she knew what was happening, Ben leaned forward and placed a soft kiss on her mouth.

# Chapter Sixteen

"Way to go, Cedar!" Ben scolded himself as he rattled around the kitchen, slapping together a peanut-butter-and-banana sandwich for his father.

"Ouch!" Al covered his ears with his hands.

"I'm sorry, Dad. I'm just a little frustrated with myself. Come sit down, please—your sandwich is ready."

As a small blessing, his father sat down without protest. His silence, except for some enthusiastic chewing, gave Ben time to think, though he wasn't sure how much thinking he was ready to do.

Why, he asked himself, had he picked then of all times to kiss her? Now she probably thought he'd played the pity card for a chance to kiss her again.

He tried to interpret the look on Frankie's

face when she'd pulled away and said, "I have to go. Rae will be waiting for me." He didn't think she looked angry or even surprised. Her cheeks had flushed pink, making her look particularly captivating, and she had searched his eyes with a myriad of questions in her own.

*Lord, where is Your direction in my life? I feel like I keep doing the wrong things.*

His father belched softly and pushed his plate away.

Ben turned to him. "Do you want another, Dad?"

"Nope!"

Ben carried the dishes to the sink and rinsed them off, and got his father settled on the couch with an assortment of seashells and small rocks to sort. He thought about making himself something for lunch, but he couldn't chase away the image of his father in the restraint chair and he had no appetite.

As well, he kept checking the time, anxious to hear word about Danny. And, pushing through both of these thoughts, the memory of his second kiss with Frankie nestled into his mind.

Frankie was grateful that Rae had asked to spend the afternoon at the library.

"We're going to be supervised, Mom," she

explained. "It's a chance for us to do extra work on our special projects. Can I *please* stay?"

Her glasses slid down her paint-smudged nose. Frankie pushed them back up for her and touched a spot of paint with a gentle finger.

"What time should I come back?"

"Hurray!" Rae set her off-kilter with an enthusiastic hug. "You're the best, Mom! Can you come back at four?"

They decided that Rae would be ready and waiting promptly at four o'clock, and Frankie was left with extra time to sort out her thoughts.

She pondered whether the summer was turning out to be what she needed and wanted it to be for her and Rae. Certainly, there were complications that she hadn't expected, but there had been unexpected joys, too. Rae seemed to be her happy, quirky and creative self again, but what about her own life? Was she really keeping her own goals in mind if her thoughts insisted on returning to Ben and to those kisses?

They had caught her off guard, but she hadn't disliked them. No, actually, it was quite the opposite. For those heady, intoxicating moments, nothing else in life had mattered apart from the sensation of Ben's warm and gentle lips on hers, bringing forth feelings she thought she'd put to rest permanently.

Then common sense had spoken jarringly

into her ear. Did she really want to put herself or Rae at risk of being hurt again? Even if she was so inclined, she knew that Ben already had all-consuming priorities.

She checked the time and wondered how long it would be before they heard word about Danny. The practical part of her said that she didn't need to get involved. Too late, she thought. All she had to do was think about Rae and her mother's heart wouldn't allow her to ignore what happened to the young boy. Besides, she couldn't bring herself to let Ben carry the extra load without doing her share.

Frankie was just passing by the Ice Cream Adventure, when she saw Ben and Al headed in her direction. No doubt, Ben was trying to help his father walk off some of his jitters in hopes of a reprieve later on.

"Oh, hi," Ben said when he saw her. His eyes searched hers anxiously, as if seeking reassurance that she wasn't upset that he had kissed her again. She mustered a smile to show him that she was fine and hoped the smile masked that inside she was still a turmoil of emotions that she didn't even want to begin to interpret.

"Where's Rae?" he asked. "I thought you had gone to pick her up?"

"They were able to keep the room longer at

the library and she has a project she wanted to keep working on."

"She sure seems to love her art," Ben observed.

"Yes, she does."

"Have you heard anything back from Irma yet?" she asked. "I mean, I know it's early, but I just wondered."

"No, nothing yet," Ben said. "Walk with us?" he urged. "If you have time."

They strolled, watching Al amble along a few steps ahead of them.

"Ah…" Ben began. "I've been meaning to talk to you about those kisses."

"They were nothing," Frankie interjected hastily.

"Nothing?" Ben raised his eyebrows at her. "Well, that's just so flattering."

She chuckled uncomfortably. "I didn't mean it like that. They were—ah—nice." She could feel her own cheeks growing warm. "I just didn't want to make too big a deal out of it."

"But isn't it a big deal?" Ben asked, growing more serious. "To show affection like that usually means something, doesn't it?"

Frankie stopped and turned to face him. "And in our case, what do you think it *could* mean?" she demanded.

Ben looked slightly taken aback. Frankie

resumed walking, and he hurried to catch up with her.

"Look," he said. "I'm not suggesting that we make this into more than what it is or can be. I just… I just wanted you to know that I'm not the kind of man who does things like that without any regard for the other person's feelings."

"So, you do that sort of thing often?"

"Frankie, you know that isn't what I meant."

She shrugged her shoulders. When Ben began to speak again she could hear the note in his voice that asked for understanding.

"I told you about my mom," he said. "And I don't share that story often. You told me about your ex-husband, and I have the feeling that's also something that has been stuck inside of you for a long time. I don't know exactly what any of that means, and I'm not in the position to make any promises but I want you to know that I won't forget the bond we shared."

Frankie couldn't even explain to herself the contrary feelings that flared up in her.

"Good to know," she said abruptly. "Listen, I just remembered I've got an errand to run. Let me know when you hear something."

She walked rapidly in the other direction, trying not to visualize what she was sure was a very puzzled look on Ben's face.

*I don't know what to do!* Frankie thought as

she walked. *I don't even know how I'm supposed to feel anymore.* She completely agreed with Ben that there was no point delving into something when circumstances prevented both of them from having the time or the inclination. So, why had it bothered her so much to hear him say that he couldn't make any promises?

Her tentatively rekindled relationship with God still felt tenuous, but she didn't know who else to share her questions with. She knew Rae was very happy here, and yet she couldn't help wondering if it would be better to put some distance between herself and Ben. She would just have to find a way to make Rae understand.

Frankie hadn't heard God's voice in her heart for a long time. She could barely remember a time when she had accepted the simple but profound fact that Jesus had died for her sins, that she was allowed to be weak so that God could be strong.

Maybe it was time to think about that again.

She rummaged through the drawers of the cabin, on the chance that there had been a Bible left like there was in hotel rooms. When she found one in a bottom drawer, it seemed clear what God wanted her to do.

She made herself a glass of iced tea and took the Bible out onto the deck, where she sat and turned pages until she found a familiar Psalm.

## Chapter Seventeen

Ben, who had been puzzled by Frankie's abrupt departure, was relieved to see her sitting and reading on her deck, and then even more pleased when he saw what she was reading. As he'd walked back home with his dad, he had replayed their conversation in his head and tried to think of what he might have said that had triggered her return to the Frankie of the folded arms and the haughty chin. He had wanted to reassure her that he had no intention of putting any pressure on her because of two kisses, no matter how enjoyable they had been. Actually, they had been more than enjoyable, Ben realized. They had opened his mind and his heart to the possibility of truly caring for a woman. He couldn't let himself, not now. But the possibility was there.

He saw Frankie register the footsteps that signaled his approach and she looked up. Although she quickly arranged her features back into neutrality, for a moment he thought he saw in her eyes that what he had meant as reassurance had somehow wounded her. Was it possible that she, too, wished that circumstances were different?

It was difficult to keep perspective on the matter when she looked so appealing with the sun shining on her bright hair. As well, seeing her read the Bible wrenched at his heart in a way he couldn't explain.

"Can I come back to talk after I get Dad settled?" Ben asked.

She looked slightly startled but nodded.

When he returned, they sat for a moment looking, but not quite looking, at each other. Ben anxiously threaded and unthreaded his fingers, and prayed that God would help him find the right words.

"When I say that I can't make any promises," he began slowly, "that doesn't mean that the kisses were meaningless to me. I just wish—" He sighed. "Well, there's no sense wishing, but in a different time and place…"

Frankie's cheeks and the tips of her ears flushed pink, but she kept her jaw rigid and fixed him with a narrow-eyed gaze.

"I don't want you to think that I don't respect

you, because I do so much. And I don't want you to think any less of me as a person," he said.

"I don't," Frankie said very quietly.

"So we're okay, then?"

She wouldn't quite look at him, but her jawline had softened.

"Yes, we're fine."

Ben gestured toward the Bible. "What prompted this, if you don't mind me asking?"

"No, I don't mind you asking, but I'm not sure how much of an answer I can give you. I—I guess I've just been thinking more about God again since I've been here. Maybe I'm just tired of being mad at Him."

"That's a good place to start," Ben said quietly.

"I actually used to love church until… Well, anyway, I'm finding my way back. Trying to find my way back," she amended.

Frankie stood up and gathered her hair into a ponytail, signaling, Ben thought, that vulnerable Frankie was gone and it was time to get back to business.

"I'm getting some apple juice. Would you like some?" she asked.

Ben nodded and felt relief surge through him that his words hadn't caused irreparable damage.

When she returned with two glasses, Ben had his phone to his ear and was listening intently.

Frankie waited, her brown eyes anxious above her glass, and she took a sip of juice.

"I see," Ben said. "Yes, I understand. Well, I guess that's what we hoped for, isn't it? Thanks for letting me know."

"Was that Irma?" Frankie asked as soon as he'd hung up the phone."

"Yes."

"And?" Frankie urged, anxiousness infusing her voice.

"The judge has agreed that community service is the best way for Danny to pay his dues. He had no priors. I gather from Irma that he's actually been a pretty good kid until his parents separated. It doesn't take a degree in psychology to see that he's acting out. And," Ben added, "why he's doing it."

Frankie nodded in agreement and her expression of concern mirrored his. "What will Danny be doing?" she asked.

"Irma said that Colin tried to convince the judge to let him take Danny back to Saskatoon, where they live, and get him lined up with some volunteer work there."

"I hope the judge didn't agree." Frankie's face crumpled into lines of worry.

"Well, the judge agreed that Colin has some rights as Danny's father," Ben said, "but it was his strong recommendation that Danny pay his recompense to the community he has harmed."

Frankie nodded vigorously. "Yes, that makes total sense. So what happens now?"

"The community is going to meet and review the damages, set some priorities and put together a list of what Danny will be assisting with. I can tell you there will be some long days ahead for that boy."

"I hope he understands how fortunate he is," Frankie said.

"I hope so, too. I pray for it."

"And will you be able to help him?" Frankie asked, "Teach him some of the skills he'll need?"

"It sounds like we'll be able to work that out," Ben said. "Also, it won't be part of his official hours, but I'm going to talk to Irma about how good Danny was with Dad and see if I can give her a bit of a reprieve by having Danny come over here sometimes. I thought that…"

Frankie's concerns on the matter showed on her face and Ben stopped what he was going to say and asked, "What's the matter?"

"How much do you think he'll be around here?" she asked, hearing her own voice betray her apprehension.

"Not all that often," Ben said. "I thought

this was a good thing? That it was the way we wanted it to work out?"

"Oh, I'm definitely happy about the community-service aspect," Frankie said. "But I don't know how much I want Danny to be around Rae—you heard the way he talked to her."

"And I heard her put him in his place pretty quickly," Ben said with a chuckle.

"True, but still…"

"We'll work it out," Ben said. "If it causes any worry or concern for you, we don't have to do it. I would never want to do anything that made you or Rae uncomfortable."

"Well, he is really good with Al," Frankie conceded. "Maybe we can see how it goes."

"We'll figure it out," Ben agreed. "I promise."

Ben asked himself why he was making promises that he really had no right to be making. It was so easy to say *we* like he and Frankie were in some kind of partnership, but what was going to happen when the summer was over? Already the days felt like they were on fast-forward, hurtling him toward the time when he had to put Al into a care facility. It wasn't fair to anyone, including himself, to focus on anything else… no matter how enticing he found Frankie, which he realized more and more that he did. Once again he reminded himself that there was no point wanting something he couldn't have...especially when he didn't deserve it.

Sadness clutched him in its dreary grip. In some ways he wished he had never met Frankie, because then he might be able to stop thinking about what he was missing.

Rae was ready and waiting for Frankie when she returned to the library at the designated time. Her forehead, cheeks and hands were sprinkled with a rainbow of paint colors, and her hair had completely given up her braids and fuzzed softly around her face. Her eyes were bright with excitement and she grinned widely.

Frankie couldn't help an answering grin to her beaming daughter.

"You look like you had a great day," she said. "And a slightly messy one."

Rae looked down at herself and appeared genuinely surprised, which made Frankie smile again, but in a more secret way.

"What did you work on?" she asked as they started to walk home. "Do you want me to carry that for you?"

Rae walked with her arms spread wide, balancing a rolled-up canvas between them.

"No, I'm good." She staggered a little, slightly out of breath.

"Are you sure?"

"Uh-huh," Rae said.

"So, what is that?" Frankie asked again. "What did you work on?"

"It's a surprise," Rae said.

Frankie nodded, then blinked in surprise when her daughter added, "It's for Al, a surprise for Al."

Frankie stopped walking. "Really?" she asked.

Rae stopped, too. "Yes," she said, shuffling with embarrassment. "I just thought he might like a picture to put up when he has to go live somewhere else. I thought it could help to make him feel at home. What's wrong, Mom?" she asked, uneasily. "Did I do something wrong?"

"No, Sweet Pea." Frankie swallowed. "You didn't do anything wrong at all. I'm just so touched that you would think of something like that."

They began to walk again. "You're right that Al will have to go live somewhere else," Frankie remarked. "How did you know that?"

"I hear people talking," Rae confessed. "A lot of people know Al and Ben, and everybody's kind of worried about them. I've heard you and Ben talking, too."

For the umpteenth time, Frankie was reminded that her daughter's young-for-her-age appearance and awkward ways masked an intuitive heart.

"When is Al going to move?" Rae asked.

"I think Ben plans to move him when summer is over," Frankie replied. "But it's not going to be easy for either of them."

"Because it will make Ben sad, right?"

Frankie nodded. "Very sad."

Rae slowed her pace again and furrowed her brow, considering. "It's hard on a person, being sad," she said, sounding suddenly years older than her actual age.

"Yes, it is," Frankie agreed, and waited.

"A while back I was sad all the time," Rae continued. "I'm not anymore."

Frankie sent up a silent prayer of thanks.

"I don't want Ben to be sad, either," Rae said. "I like Ben, I just…" She shrugged and averted her eyes, returning to the ten-year-old that she was.

"I know, Rae. I understand."

Maybe, Frankie thought, with God's help, there was a chance that her friendship with Ben could last beyond the summer. But did that mean she was admitting that she *wanted* it to?

Back at their cabin, Rae carefully unfurled the picture she had made for Al and spread it out on the kitchen table for Frankie to look at.

It was not a professional work of art, by any means. It was the work of a gifted child, but still unmistakably the work of a child. Yet, Rae had captured the rustic look of the cabins, the majesty of the pines, and the tempestuous grays and blues of the sky.

"Do you think Al will like it?" she asked.

"I think he will love it," Frankie said. "And I think he's very fortunate to have a friend like you who cares so much about him."

"Maybe we can go visit him," Rae suggested. "I mean wherever he ends up living."

"Maybe so," Frankie said, not wanting to make a promise she couldn't keep. "Now, you must be hungry. What should we make?"

"Hot dogs! Or maybe grilled cheese sandwiches?"

"Okay, let's get your picture off the table so that nothing happens to it."

As they tidied up and got things ready for an early supper, Frankie thought how nice it would be if she was able to tell Rae that for sure they would visit Al.

She let her mind wander as she buttered bread and got out cheese slices. What if she and Ben actually did keep in touch after the time at the lake was over? Regina and Saskatoon weren't an unreasonable distance apart, and these days, distances could be easily overcome by phone, text, email and Facebook.

What did it all mean, she wondered, as she rummaged in the cupboard for a can of tomato soup. Why did it suddenly matter to her that they keep in touch?

Was it possible that her heart was actually starting to open to Ben?

Frankie thought about everything Ben had done for them. She thought about his love for his father, and the dignity and respect he afforded him as Alzheimer's gnawed at the older man's mind. She thought about his natural relationship with God and the way it had helped her come to terms with her own struggles. And she thought about those kisses…

*What happens next?* she prayed. Was God trying to tell her that she would have to be satisfied just to know her heart could be brought back to life? But a sudden image of Ben's blue eyes sent her emotions spiraling again.

Rae hummed under her breath as she carefully folded two paper napkins and laid one by each plate. Frankie arranged carrot sticks and tomatoes on a plate.

"So, Danny had court today," Frankie said, feeling her daughter out on the subject.

"What happened?" Rae asked, pausing with a spoon clutched in her hand. "Does he have to go to jail?"

"No, thankfully. The judge decided that he could have the chance to apologize to the community by helping with work that needs to be done around here."

Rae considered this and nodded, placing the spoon down by her bowl. "That's good, then."

"That *is* good," Frankie agreed. "Rae...how would you feel about Danny being over at Ben's cabin in the evenings sometimes?"

"What for?" Rae questioned in a suspicious tone.

"Ben thinks he might be some help with Al. They seemed to get along pretty well, didn't you think?"

"I get along with Al!" Rae declared, folding her arms. "And I can help him."

"Yes, that's very true but..."

At that moment, an exclamation of dismay from outside caught Frankie's attention and she hurried to the door in time to see Ben rush out of his cabin, wearing oven mitts and clutching a pan that teemed with flames.

Frankie gasped and rushed outside, but Ben, acting quickly, had grabbed a nearby garden hose and doused the flames.

"What happened?" Frankie cried. Rae had come outside, too, to see what all of the commotion was.

"I fell asleep," Ben said. Guilt and fatigue

hung on his face, and Frankie felt an ache for him that went right into her bones.

"I fell asleep," he said again. "And Dad decided he would try to make supper."

## Chapter Eighteen

Ben read the sympathy that struggled with the fear on Frankie's face and it didn't help him to feel any better. Rae had her hands clapped over her mouth and again reminded him of the timid little girl he had first met.

He could only imagine the sight he had made as he fled the cabin, carrying the burning pot like an unwelcome offering.

He didn't know why he should feel guilty and embarrassed—he hadn't done it. However, he was the one who had fallen asleep and, in that regard, he was responsible.

He didn't dare imagine how much worse it could have been, and the shock of it kept his prayers coiled away from thanking God that it hadn't been worse. He couldn't get past thinking that it was bad enough it had happened in the first place.

"What can I do to help?" Frankie's quiet voice broke through his churning thoughts.

Ben looked at her and saw that she had willfully steadied herself and pushed her own feelings behind a professional, compassionate demeanor.

"Is Al okay?" Rae whispered. She hugged herself like her stomach ached.

"Yes, he's okay," Ben answered her first, then turned to Frankie.

"I don't think there's anything to be done now. Dad's sitting in the cabin, probably wondering what I'm doing out here and what happened to his supper."

Ben heard the slight resentment in his voice, and he quickly prayed to rid himself of it. But, the thing was, he was just plain tired in all kinds of ways, and today's incident was a glaring, potentially dangerous reminder of that.

"I suppose," he said. "I'd better get back to him."

"I'm making soup and sandwiches," Frankie said. "Why don't I bring some over?"

"Thanks, but I'm not sure how hungry I am."

"You don't have to eat." Her brown eyes were filled with concern. "But I don't think you should be alone."

How was it, Ben wondered, that this summer had turned into such a different experience from the one he had hoped for? Or expected? On the one hand, his hopes of forming new memories at Silver Lake with his father seemed to have been shattered. But, on the other hand, this wonderful, strong and spirited woman and her awkward, creative daughter had touched his summer in such a way that he could hardly remember a time when he hadn't known them.

He couldn't put that into words and didn't even know what it meant. So, he simply said, "That would be nice, thank you."

The next day it poured rain and the sky was illuminated with lightning.

"Ow!" Al declared loudly with each clap of thunder. "Stop it!" he raged, shaking his fist at the sky.

"Ah, Dad," Ben sighed. "Have you decided you're not even going to be friends with God anymore?"

He tried to get his father occupied with his seashells, but it was to no avail, as the noise of the storm kept him too agitated to sit still. Ben, unable to focus on anything of his own because of his father's restlessness, was seriously contemplating the repercussions of cutting the holiday short. He was sure that his dad wouldn't mind—or even really know or care. The near miss tragedy with the burning pan had convinced Ben that he was only fooling himself if he thought he could continue to take care of his father. He needed to get them both home, back to a familiar environment and start making the necessary arrangements.

But his heart urged him not to forget that he had felt led to help Danny pay his dues, and there had to be a reason for that, even if the only reason was because he understood what it was like to be a teenage boy with bigger questions than there seemed to be answers for, so sometimes things felt like they wanted to explode and come spilling out.

But it was more than that. Much as he wanted to fight it or deny it, he knew that it was more. He didn't want to disappoint Frankie or Rae, not in any way. He had already dreaded the end of summer, and now he had another goodbye coming that he wasn't in any way prepared for. He couldn't stand the thought of it coming any sooner than it absolutely had to.

He and Frankie had a conversation by calling out through their kitchen windows and agreed that it wasn't exactly weather for sitting on the deck and drinking coffee. Frankie said that Rae had been distraught for five minutes over her art class being canceled, but had quickly rallied with the temptation of cinnamon toast and hot chocolate for breakfast and the chance to look at her art books all day, or at least until the rain let up, if it ever decided to.

"Hot chocolate and leisurely reading time," Ben said. "That does sound tempting. I don't suppose she has any Batman comics?"

"Um, doubtful," Frankie said, pretending to take his request seriously. "I'll check and get back to you."

Ben liked this playful side of Frankie very much, and he was glad that he'd had some opportunity to see her sense of humor.

The laughter stilled in him as he realized that he actually missed her. They were separated by only a wet, sludgy path and already he missed her. How was that possible? Only a short time ago she had been a stranger to him, and now he didn't want to be apart from her. Once again he pushed back the thought of summer's end and briefly allowed himself to savor the possibility of continuing to get to know Frankie afterward.

There was a Psalm that said that God would open His hand and give us the desires of our heart. Ben had always thought that meant that if his wishes were aligned with God's will, then the Lord would work with him to help them come true. Now he wondered if it could mean that God would give him the desires of his heart, in that He would teach him how much he wanted something—or someone—that he hadn't even known he had wanted.

The previous night, after the fire incident, Frankie and Rae had come over, bearing soup and sandwiches for which Ben found he'd had more of an appetite than he'd anticipated. As he talked things through with Frankie, while Rae sat at the table with Al and made rows of stones with him, Ben began to feel something that he had not expected to feel—security and comfort. He couldn't help allowing himself to wish for a moment that they could pursue a real relationship.

"Stop!" his father raged at the thunder, snapping Ben back into the present. Al trembled from head to foot, wound tight with agitation.

Ben stood beside him and tried to take his hand, but Al shook it off.

"It's okay, Dad," Ben said, doing his best to soothe with his voice, instead. "It's okay."

Frankie had brought him a reprieve last night, which had caused some pleasant speculation. But now, Ben mused sadly, a storm still raged outside—and within his father—and much as he might wish otherwise, there were still no easy answers.

One thing he could do, he thought, was try again to reach Danny's grandmother to find out when and where Danny was scheduled to start his volunteer work and find out if the boy was willing to take some pointers from him.

He got through to Irma, who was glad to hear from him and, after confirming a few things, handed the phone to her grandson. Danny sounded considerably subdued, but not sullen, and actually mumbled a thank-you when Ben said he could teach him some things that would make the work go more smoothly. They agreed to meet at the Nature Center, the site of the worst damage, early the next morning. Ben reasoned with himself that his dad would likely still be asleep and he would ask Frankie if she wouldn't mind sticking close by. He regretted having to ask her but couldn't see another way.

Ben stood in the doorway of their cabin and looked across at Frankie's through the barrier of pounding rain. *We need Your help, Lord*, he prayed, as, behind him, his father paced and spewed harsh words.

*Please God*, Frankie prayed. *Help me know what I'm supposed to do.*

After the emergency with the burning pot had interrupted her talk with Rae about Danny spending time with Al, she hadn't known how to raise the subject again. But, as she prayed about that, she acknowledged that it was far from being the only thing on her mind and heart, although she certainly hadn't intended to let her blue-eyed summer neighbor play havoc with her heart. She knew that hadn't been Ben's intention, either. Maybe he wasn't feeling the same things about her—she knew he was kind by nature... Yet, he had kissed her, not just once but twice, and she dared to think that it wasn't simply her imagination when a certain soft light came into his eyes.

Frankie reminded herself yet again that the timing was bad for both of them, but then she remembered that the Bible said there was a time and season for everything, and she considered the possibility that they should be following the Lord's timing, not their own.

She also realized that, with Ben's encouragement, she was rediscovering her own traits of strength and commitment. After Trevor left, she had forgotten those things about herself and it felt very good to unearth them again.

She had come to Silver Lake to find healing, and it felt like she was well on her way to finding it...and perhaps more. She murmured a heartfelt thank-you.

"Who are you talking to, Mom?" Rae had returned to her art and had been working happily on it, unmindful of the battering elements outside.

"I'm talking to God." Frankie reached out an

arm and scooped Rae into a side hug. It felt so good to say that.

"Oh, okay." Rae nodded sagely. "He's pretty nice to talk to."

Frankie laughed and squeezed Rae tighter, breathing in the scents of waxy crayons, chocolate and cinnamon, until her daughter protested and wiggled away.

"Oh, I thought about Danny spending time with Al," Rae said breezily over her shoulder as she perused the fridge for a snack.

"And?" Frankie prompted cautiously.

"I guess it would be okay, but I think I should be there to keep an eye on things."

Frankie smiled, once again feeling profoundly grateful. "I'm sure we can figure something out. Thanks, Sweet Pea. You're a good person."

Rae took a huge bite into an apple and nodded. She chewed, swallowed and said, "I like to think so." She added, "I'm bored. I wish it would stop raining."

"Me, too," Frankie admitted. "Should we play a card game or something?"

They had just started to deal out the cards for a game of crazy eights when Rae suddenly went very still and tilted her head.

"Listen," she whispered. "Do you hear?"

"What?" Frankie asked.

"Hear the quiet? I think it's stopped raining!"

She flew to the door and flung it open, and cried excitedly over her shoulder, "It stopped! It stopped raining!"

She threw her arms open wide, as if to embrace the world.

"It smells great out here, Mom. Can I go outside?"

Frankie laughed. "I guess so. Make sure you put something on your feet, though. It will be mucky out there."

Rae quickly obeyed and was soon outside, clomping merrily in puddles.

It seemed to Frankie that the way the storm had raged and then just as quickly dissipated reminded her of the way her dark feelings had begun to flee, even though she had felt they would never leave her.

She didn't want to become too preoccupied with the activity in the other cabin, but she guessed that Ben and Al would be out the door soon, as the older man would be more than ready to break free from the cabin. She could only imagine how the past few hours had gone with them cooped up inside while a disruptive storm raged around them.

Sure enough, it wasn't long before they appeared on their deck. Frankie saw Ben notice her and wave. She waved back, and he beckoned for her to come outside.

"Sorry for getting you outside in this mess of mud," he said when she reached him. "But the temptation of a friendly face was too much."

"That's okay," Frankie said, glad that he'd waved her over. "I imagine it wasn't very much fun being cooped up with your dad."

"Not so much, no."

Ben knelt to tie Al's shoes for him and said, "I trust you ladies got along all right?"

"We did. I had a chance to talk to Rae about Danny spending time with you and Al."

Ben stood up. "Oh, really? What did she say?"

"At first she wasn't any too keen on the idea."

"I can understand that," Ben said.

"But she must have taken some time to think it over," Frankie continued. "Because later she told me that she was okay with it. *Provided*," she emphasized with some amusement, "that she be close by to make sure things go okay."

"I wouldn't have it any other way," Ben said, catching the amusement. He added in a more serious tone, "She's a wonderful girl, Frankie. She really is."

Frankie's eyes found Rae, who already had smudges of mud on both of her knees and a tiny, water-saturated twig lodged in her braid.

Frankie sighed and shook her head, her heart

clenched in love for her funny girl. Rae beamed back the sun in her wide smile.

She turned back to Ben and had to swallow a lump in her throat when she saw the pure, open affection on his face. Here was a man who was not only kind to her but who truly cared about her daughter.

"Hey," he said gently, "you okay?"

Frankie nodded and smiled. "Yes, I'm more than okay—I'm great."

Ben squeezed both of her hands quickly and gently in his and said, "That makes me happy."

Rae did a splashing dance over to them and announced that her next picture was going to be called *After the Rain* and then gleefully twirled through a puddle.

If she had seen them holding hands, it did not appear to concern her in any way and Frankie felt even larger gems being strung on her necklace of hope.

## Chapter Nineteen

Bright and early the next morning, Ben and Danny stood surveying the graffiti on the side of the Nature Center. To his credit, Danny looked thoroughly ashamed. Ben could only imagine how it must feel to face that angry piece of artwork in broad daylight with another person gauging it with you and without the cloak of anonymity.

But it was time to get down to business. "Okay," he said to Danny, "here's how we're going to start…" Ben's hope was that it wouldn't take long to get the boy confident enough to work on his own so that Ben could pop back to check on his dad. Even though Frankie had assured him that she would be fine with Al for as long as was needed, he didn't feel right about neglecting his duties to his father for any length of time.

Ben sighed and wondered if he would have that cloud hanging over him for the rest of his life: the feeling that no matter how much he did, it would never quite make up for what he hadn't done. And the fact that he would never be able to hear from his father's own mouth that he was forgiven for not making it home before Mom died.

For the longest time, he had felt that was his burden to carry and he hadn't even considered the possibility of sharing it with anyone else. Then Frankie had come along and he knew that, despite his best efforts to push any feelings away, something in him was beginning to change, and his yearning to open up and share his entire burden was growing stronger.

"Like this?" Danny's question interrupted his thoughts and Ben turned to see him awkwardly clutching a paintbrush like it was about to fly out of his hand and take on a life of its own.

"Maybe just move your hand down a bit, like this." Ben showed him. "Hold it firmly but don't choke the life out of it." He winked at Danny, who looked startled and then chuckled reluctantly.

"Come on," Ben said. "I'll show you how it's done and when you feel you're ready, you can give it a go on your own. Sound fair?"

Danny nodded. They worked side by side

with Ben coaching and encouraging. He noticed the way the boy straightened his slumped shoulders and how he applied each stroke of paint with a bit more confidence and precision than the one before. He guessed that Danny hadn't received much praise or encouragement lately and it was good to see a glimmer of the positive impact it could have.

"Gran says I'm supposed to thank you and your family for helping me," Danny mumbled when they stopped to drink some water.

Ben thought about correcting him and explaining that he and Al were a family and that Frankie and Rae were a different family with no connection. But he found that the words stuck in his throat and ached. He took a sip of water and gave the boy's shoulder a brief, friendly squeeze. "Ready to get back at it?"

After another hour or so of working together, Ben introduced Danny to a couple of other workers who he knew would treat the boy fairly but firmly. He felt bad about leaving, but he had to know how his father was getting along and there was no sense denying that he wanted to see Frankie, too.

When he got back to the cabins, Frankie was on his deck sipping from a cup. As he drew closer, he could smell the soothing, refreshing smell of peppermint.

Ben had the thought that the sight of her, with the sun and shadow playing games on her finely boned face, brought its own comfort, and he found he wanted to pause and watch her, as she watched his father and Rae splashing in the puddles that were left over from rain.

Al chortled as his stomping foot sent a splash of mud flying in all directions. Rae gleefully stomped a muddy retort.

"Looks like we'll both be hitting up the laundromat," Ben observed as he approached the deck.

Frankie's face lit with a smile that caused a shift within him. It wasn't a bad feeling, not at all. It was just one that he wasn't entirely familiar with.

"You're back!" she said. "How did it go?"

"Danny's trying hard." Ben eased himself into the other chair. "I believe he wants to do well. He, ah…" Ben hesitated, feeling inept at expressing himself.

"He what?" Frankie asked.

"He said to say thank you—he said his grandma wanted him to thank me and my family."

Frankie looked perplexed at his discomfiture, and then understanding altered her expression into one that reflected her own uncertainty.

"You explained to him that we're not a family?" she asked.

Ben shrugged and shook his head. "I didn't want to complicate things by getting into it."

"I see," Frankie said softly, after a moment, in a tone that he couldn't decipher.

He prayed briefly for the right words.

"Frankie," he said. "Lately, maybe I have found myself wishing things could be different—wishing that maybe we could have pursued something, at least an ongoing friendship, but my situation with Dad is not going to change."

Emotion flared brightly on Frankie's face.

"I know that," she said, in a steely, calm voice. "And I have Rae. I don't recall doing or saying anything to make you think that I asked or expected anything of you."

The proclamations hung between them, and Ben wondered if they were preparing each other—and themselves—for the inevitable separation.

They turned their attention to the mud frolickers. Frustration and regret swirled like a tidal wave through Ben. He didn't know why the words that left his mouth never seemed to convey what he was really feeling inside. Maybe it was because he didn't know himself what he truly wanted. To his surprise it was Frankie who murmured under her breath, "I'm sorry," and gave his hand a quick squeeze.

"You don't have to be." Ben squeezed back.

"I understand about your father," she said. "Trust me, I really do." Color rose in her cheeks again as she added, "And I admit I wasn't expecting to have as strong a connection with you as I do. Trust me when I say that's the last thing in the world that was even on my radar when we came here."

She paused, and her face told Ben that it was important to her that he understood what she was saying.

"I couldn't imagine that I'd even *want* to be friends with a man after what my ex-husband did to me." Here her voice splintered before she gathered herself again. "But I want you to know that I am glad that I've had the chance to get to know you."

Ben squeezed her hand again. "I appreciate that. I do believe that God lets things happen for a reason, even if the reason is just to help each other through a brief passage of time in our lives."

Frankie's expression was reflective. "I suppose I'm starting to believe again that God has His reasons," she said thoughtfully. "But I think sometimes those reasons just make me ask more questions."

"I don't think any of us ever get past having questions," Ben said. "I think that the fact that we keep seeking answers is what faith is all about."

Frankie nodded slowly. "That's another thing I wasn't sure I'd ever find again," she said.

"Mom," Rae called over to them. "Al and I want to go for ice cream."

"Oh, Al and you, is that right?" Frankie teased.

"That sounds like a good plan to me," Ben said as he dug in his pockets for money. "My treat."

The weather favored them by staying warm and sunny, and after they got their ice cream, they continued to the beach. Ben and Frankie sat and watched as Al and Rae slowly patrolled the edge of the water looking for treasure.

"They're a good team," Frankie said.

"So are we," Ben said, then darted a glance at her, hoping she would grasp the spirit he'd said it in. She didn't respond, but she didn't look upset, either.

Sleep had only taunted Frankie and she was out of bed early. Despite being tired, she chose to make peppermint tea, as she was sure that caffeine would only contribute to her already jangled nerves. All night conflicting thoughts about Ben had gone through her head, not in an orderly march but in a jumble of flips and backward somersaults. Despite the calm, accepting exterior that she showed him, her emotions were in turmoil as she anguished over what it meant for God to bring Ben Cedar into her life and to show her it was possible to have feelings again, only to remove him a short time later.

She visualized the affectionate, probing expression in his eyes when he looked at her. She recalled the softness of his lips, and felt pleasure when she thought of his lopsided grin. But it was the person he was—his character and integrity—that she knew she would miss most of all.

Carefully and quietly, so she wouldn't wake Rae, Frankie took her tea and the Bible out to the deck. She opened it to Proverbs, and then just sat, with one hand resting lightly on it and the other one curved around her cup, letting the cool morning breeze and the scent of peppermint smooth away her tumbling thoughts.

Ben's cabin was dark and quiet, and she wondered what kind of night he'd had and what projects he would help Danny with today. Ben had said that he didn't want to tie Frankie down to staying close by for his father every day, so he'd made arrangements for one of their family friends to sit with him for a while. Frankie had told him she didn't mind, but he insisted.

Morning meditations were becoming a habit again with Frankie, and she included Danny in her prayers now, as well as her usual prayers that the Lord would continue to protect and guide Rae and her, as well as to uphold Ben as he dealt with the daily challenges of caregiving.

A couple of hours later Rae yawned and spooned cereal into her mouth as she slumped in her chair.

"Sit up, please," Frankie said.

Rae gave a slow, lazy turtle blink and straightened up in her chair.

"When is Danny going to come over?" she asked around a mouthful of cereal.

"Chew and swallow, please," Frankie said. "And I'm not sure. That's up to Ben."

"Or we could invite him over."

"Do you want to?" Frankie asked, surprised.

"We could," Rae said. "He's not that much fun right now, I don't think, but I wasn't either before doing art made me remember how to be happy again. So maybe he has poten…" Her face scrunched as she got the word out. "Potential."

"Maybe he does," Frankie agreed, tucking in her smile. "You're a good kid, Sweet Pea."

"Can I have some hot chocolate with breakfast then, please?"

"No, we save that for stormy days." Frankie crossed over and kissed her daughter's hair.

"You, miss, need a shampoo."

"I've been concentrating on my art," Rae said solemnly.

Frankie chuckled. "I see. That reminds me— did you give Al the special picture you made for him?"

Rae shrugged. "I took it over. Ben said Al was out of sorts, but he'd be sure to show it to him later."

"He will," Frankie said. "If Ben says he will, he will."

"You think he's the *greatest*." Rae crinkled her nose, but before Frankie could answer, she began spooning cereal again, satisfied with her declaration.

After Rae had scampered off to get ready for art class, Frankie considered the truth of her words. There was no doubt that she had become attached to Ben in ways that she had not antici- pated, and she was still trying her best to fight those feelings because it wouldn't do any good to prolong or develop them. Sure, there was an abundance of ways to keep in touch over dis- tance these days, but the fact of the matter was that Ben hadn't given her any indication that he had the desire to continue their contact. Instead, he had made it abundantly clear more than once that he had enough to deal with without adding a new relationship into the mix.

Frankie sharply shook her head as if the thought was an image on an Etch A Sketch that she had to erase. Ben was not the only one who had neither the time nor the circumstances for a relationship.

So why did she have to keep reminding herself?

"I'm ready to go, Mom." Rae came out of her room and Frankie was grateful for the reprieve from her speculations.

"Okay, Sweet Pea. Off we go."

After she dropped Rae off, Frankie decided to walk by the Nature Center. She thought maybe she'd find Lydia, the center volunteer whom she hadn't seen in a while. But her heart told her that what she truly wanted to do was to find Ben and see how he and Danny were getting along.

As she approached the building, she noted that the fresh paint that adorned parts of it already made it look ten times better. Then, almost immediately, she spotted Ben with Danny and something peculiar happened to her heartbeat as another, much larger, piece of scar tissue disappeared.

The boy was looking at Ben with an expression of rapt attention while Ben demonstrated the use of a smaller paint brush, gently dabbing it into a corner, then replenishing the brush and giving it to Danny to try.

*Oh, Lord, he would make such a good father...*

*Family*—the word sounded in Frankie's heart like the verse of an unfinished song.

## *Chapter Twenty*

About a week later, Ben asked Irma's permission to have Danny over for supper.

"By all means, if you want to have him," Irma said, sounding startled. "I hope he's been behaving at the work site?"

"He's doing great," Ben assured her. "He listens well and catches on very quickly. Others have said so, too."

Irma thanked him and they made arrangements that Ben would bring Danny back no later than nine o'clock.

As they walked to the cabins together, Danny chatted about the work they had done that day and Ben could tell from the boy's tone that he was proud of what they had accomplished. It was almost like he had forgotten he was paying his dues and was simply excited about the work itself. Although he had relapses, he had already come quite a ways from the bitter, sullen boy they had first met.

*Thank You, Lord*, Ben prayed, *for the work You do in people...even when they don't know You're working.*

But, the truth was, he was having a very difficult time these days figuring out exactly how God was working in his own life. He had always thought he was managing okay by keeping his focus on his dad and not fretting about what he himself might be missing. He had long ago convinced himself that this was the way things had to be. Sure, there were lonely moments and moments of wondering what-if, but, for the most part, those feelings were easy enough to keep at bay.

Then Frankie and Rae had been dropped unexpectedly into his life, and each day his acceptance of the status quo was challenged.

There was no denying that Frankie captured many of his thoughts as the days went by—and her bright, sunlit hair, expressive brown eyes and those soft, soft lips were only part of it. More often than not—and, somehow, this was even more confusing—he found himself thinking about the way she lifted her chin when she was being stubborn, the way she spoke to Rae with such utter love and the deepest kind of acceptance, and the way he could see more and more easily the way her vulnerabilities lurked beneath her aloof exterior. Yet, she pushed on and did her best to live the life she wanted to live.

But the question remained why. Why had the Lord brought someone into his life who was possibly changing the very core of what he felt he could live with—or without—if there was no purpose to it? And Ben didn't see how there could possibly be a purpose, not for him.

"Will she?" Danny's anxious voice broke into his voice as they neared the cabins.

"Sorry, Danny," Ben said, "I got a little lost in thought there. Will who what?"

"Will your wife mind that I'm coming for supper?"

Ben's heart played ping-pong. Clearly he couldn't let Danny go on thinking that he and Frankie were married, or even in a relationship.

"Danny, Frankie isn't my wife," Ben said. "As a matter of fact I didn't even know her before this summer. She and her daughter, Rae, are staying at the cabin across from ours."

He suddenly thought about how he and Frankie had met on that first day and how the boy who had wreaked the havoc was about to be his dinner guest. The Lord was either the most masterful chess player of all time, Ben thought wryly, or He had a very interesting sense of humor.

Danny shook his head slowly back and forth, with a flabbergasted look on his face. "That's so weird," he mumbled.

"What is?"

"Oh, nothin'." Danny shrugged awkwardly.

Ben put his hand on the boy's shoulder. "Danny, if there's something on your mind I want you to feel free to say it."

"Well…" the boy said slowly, "it's just that when you were at Gran's I wished that my mom and dad got along like you guys did."

The words hit a chord in Ben that he had not fully known he had but was becoming increasingly familiar with.

Danny shook his head back and forth again. "You really just met this summer?"

"We did," Ben affirmed.

"Weird… But you like her, right?"

Ben was saved from having to answer when the subject of their discussion came out onto the deck to greet them.

"Al's had a good afternoon," Frankie said, before Ben could ask. "Rae's inside with him setting the table. Hi Danny, welcome. Come on in."

Frankie had her hair piled up messily on her head, wore cutoffs and a lime-green blouse, and had what looked like a dab of salad dressing on one cheek. But something about the sight of her standing in the doorway of his cabin, greeting a guest like she belonged there, caused Ben's breath to catch.

*I do like her*, Ben silently answered Danny's question. *I like her very much.*

"Thanks again for staying with Dad," Ben said as he followed her inside. "I don't know what I'd do without you."

His words swung in the air between them and seemed to echo back to him, but Frankie didn't break her stride into the kitchen.

"I enjoy doing it," she offered over her shoulder as she scrubbed her hands at the kitchen sink. "The more I'm with your dad, the more I'm convinced that I need to get more education so I can do more—help more." Her eyes lit up with an inner determination. "I feel sometimes like a person could keep learning forever and I can't wait to start."

"You can do it, Frankie," Ben encouraged, thoroughly enjoying the way her self-confidence had blossomed. "I know that you can do anything you set your mind to."

Her cheeks flushed slightly in the way he loved. "Thanks," she said. She added flippantly, as if quenching her own pleasure in his compliments, "Everyone can use a good cheerleader in their lives. Here—" she stepped to one side

"——I'll let you get at the sink. Rae, how's the table coming along?"

"Good," Rae said. "I set it all by myself." She directed this addendum to Danny, who had joined Al in the activity of folding napkins.

"Well, goody for you," Danny drawled.

Ben sensed Frankie going into feisty mode and preparing for battle. He managed to catch her eye with a look that said, *Let's just see how this plays out.*

"You know," Rae replied in a surprisingly calm voice. "You don't have to be so mean."

The boy looked slightly startled, obviously not getting the reaction he had hoped for. Ben exchanged another glance with Frankie and saw that her concern had been replaced by curiosity seasoned with a dollop of amusement.

"My mom explained to me that when people feel bad about something, sometimes they want to say and do things that make other people feel bad, too," Rae went on in her clear, bright voice. "My parents are divorced, too," she informed the boy, who now looked shell-shocked. "But you don't see me doing and saying stupid things."

"Rae!" Frankie cautioned automatically. But Ben could tell she was struggling not to laugh. He was feeling much the same way. This time they were very careful *not* to look at each other.

*Lord, is this what it would feel like if we were watching our own kids bicker and trying to be firm when we thought something was funny?*

Wow, Danny's remarks had really got inside his head, Ben thought.

"I could show you my art," Rae said.

Danny hesitated and darted a look around the room like he was seeking help.

"Uh…sure," he said.

After securing Frankie's permission, Rae dashed back to her own cabin and returned with a couple of small pieces: a chipmunk contemplating the peanut it held between its paws with its head at a saucy angle and a ladybug making its way up the underside of the leaf.

Danny looked at the pictures and Frankie and Ben watched as his reluctance slowly turned to interest and admiration.

"You're good!" he exclaimed.

"I am," Rae agreed calmly.

She began to point out some particular facets that she wanted Danny to notice, and soon they were engrossed in conversation as if they had always been friends.

"Your girl is something," Ben said under his breath to Frankie, who turned to him then with what seemed like his own thoughts echoed in her eyes—life was full of surprises and you just never knew for sure how things were going to turn out.

He wondered if God was trying to tell him something.

The evening had passed quickly and pleasantly enough. They had enjoyed barbecued steak, accompanied by foil packets of vegetables and baked potatoes. Danny had eaten with enthusiasm and had shown that he had learned some manners somewhere along the line after all, with plenty of "please" and "thank you." It had been a delightful surprise to watch Rae and Danny bond and talk openly about a number of things, and between the two of them they had kept Al content and occupied. Yes, Frankie felt like the Lord's hand had definitely been in that gathering.

So, why was she feeling disgruntled the next day?

While Al, Rae and Danny had hovered over a puzzle at the table, she and Ben had been in the kitchen doing the dishes. Frankie had just been thinking that it felt both painfully and pleasantly domestic, when Ben had told her what Danny had said about them. He hadn't looked at her when he'd said it and, at first, she didn't look at him. But she knew that the hand holding the towel on a dish had stilled and it seemed for a moment that they had both stopped breathing. And when they had finally looked at each other, the questions in his eyes had belied the light tone he was striving for.

But she still didn't know what answers he was looking for or if she would be able to give them.

After a pause, Ben had snapped back into motion, putting the dish away in the cupboard above his head and talking about paint color choices. And, somehow, Frankie had felt she'd been offered a delicious dessert, but the plate had been snatched away before she could decide if she wanted it or not.

After she had dropped Rae off at class, listening with a distracted ear to how she was going to teach Danny to draw noses, she picked up a coffee at the Beachfront Confectionery bakery and sat at a bench by the water.

*Lord, I thought I knew what I wanted—and what I didn't want. But I'm not sure anymore. Please be a light to my pathway.*

"You look deep in thought."

Frankie started at the voice, then laughed at herself.

"You caught me asking the Lord to make sense of something for me," she told Lydia, who studied her with an interested look.

Lydia gave a grunt of acceptance and sat

down on the bench. "Well, that can be a good idea sometimes. Want to talk about it?"

"I appreciate the offer, but I wouldn't even know where to start. How's it going at the center?" Frankie asked, to change the subject.

"Pretty good," Lydia said. "I actually volunteered to come down here to get coffee for the workers because it looked like such a beautiful morning, and then I spotted you and wanted to say hi."

"It is a beautiful morning," Frankie agreed. Silently, though, she thought the air had the slight, almost indecipherable note that signaled the change of weather in August, and had, even as a child, made her ache with small regrets she didn't understand.

She swallowed and asked, "How's Danny getting along?"

"Surprisingly well," Lydia said. "It's obvious he feels terrible about what he did and he really wants to learn. And, of course, Ben is a huge help to him. He's a very decent guy, that Ben. But *you* know that…"

Frankie felt her face grow warm as scrutiny narrowed Lydia's eyes. This was followed by a light of understanding.

"That's what you're thinking about!" Lydia declared. "Or I should say *who*."

"I'm not…" Frankie protested feebly.

"Oh, come on, Frankie. If you think your face is anything but an open book, you'd better think again. Besides, it's pretty clear to anyone who sees the two of you together that you're crazy about each other."

For a brief flash, Frankie felt as if a candle had been lit inside her, shedding light, spreading warmth. Then she recalled the reality of the situation.

"Well, it doesn't matter," she said, hearing the stiffness and the self-protective dismissal in her own voice. "Ben has his own things going on with his dad and, besides, despite what you think you see, he's never said anything to me. I expect we'll go our separate ways at the end of summer and that will be that."

"But have you said anything to him?" Lydia asked.

The question caused Frankie to do an inner stumble.

"Have I said anything to…?"

"Have you told Ben how you feel? Have you said that you *want* to see where this goes after the summer?"

"I… I don't know what I really want." Frankie shook her head.

"I think you do know," Lydia prodded, in her blunt but well-meaning way. "You know, Frankie, not all men are created equal, and you can't spend the rest of your life judging the merits of all on the mistakes of one."

"I do know Ben's a good guy," Frankie agreed. "I know he's probably exactly the kind of guy I'd be looking for—if I was looking. But the timing is all wrong." She watched the hand that wasn't holding her coffee flail with frustration and she willed it to be still.

"You know what I think?" Lydia said. "I think that there are situations when we have to make our own timing. And I think that if you don't make the time to talk to Ben—I mean really talk—about how you're both feeling and see if you can get something figured out, you'll always regret it. Listen, I have to run. But think about what I said, okay?"

Frankie nodded mutely, feeling like she'd been dashed with a cold, bracing bucket of water.

She spent the rest of the day in a futile attempt to keep her mind occupied enough to not have to give Lydia's words serious consideration. But they had nestled into her mind as snugly and determinedly as a bear in its cave getting ready for winter, and by the time she picked Rae up from art class, she knew there was no getting around it: she would never be at peace in her own mind until she sat down with Ben and they decided together what—if anything—they wanted from each other when summer was over.

"You know we're only here for a couple more weeks," she couldn't help mentioning to Rae, as if she was practicing for her conversation with Ben.

"I know," Rae said breezily. "It'll be kind of a bummer, but I'm getting everybody's email addresses and my art instructor is going to call a friend of hers in Regina and make sure I keep getting help with my art."

"That sounds great," Frankie murmured as they crossed a street, being mindful of cyclists.

"Does Ben have email?" Rae asked suddenly.

"I'm sure he does."

There hadn't been any talk of sharing supper that evening, and Frankie was just as glad to have relative quiet to try to prepare what she would say to Ben. Thankfully, Rae was easy to please, and they were eating soup and sandwiches together when there was a tap on their cabin door.

Rae jumped up to get the door and announced, "Mom, it's Ben."

Frankie stood up and wiped her moist hands on her shorts, feeling suddenly nervous.

But as soon as she saw the look on his face, any thought of having a meaningful talk about their future immediately fled.

"What's wrong?" she asked. "Is it your dad?"

"No, no," Ben quickly reassured her. "He's fine, but I would like to talk to you about something. I'm sorry to interrupt your supper."

"Oh no, that's fine. Come in."

"I won't stay long. Danny came back with me again and he's with Dad."

"Should Rae…?"

"No, I think it's fine if she hears this," Ben said. "Hi, Rae."

"Hi, Ben."

"Come sit down." Frankie jittered, pulling out another kitchen chair.

"What is it?" she asked.

"I had a phone call from Irma today," Ben said. "She heard from Colin and he's decided that he's going to talk to the judge again and take Danny back with him to Saskatoon. Colin will be here in two days."

"Can he do that?" Frankie asked. Rae stirred her spoon through her soup, listening.

"Apparently so," Ben said, one hand agitating his hair. "The courts released him to the care of a parent and/or guardian and there was no stipulation on where the volunteer work had to be completed, only the judge's recommendation."

"But it only makes sense to have it completed here," Frankie protested. "And Danny is doing so well with you and with everything. I feel he actually has a chance to really change here, not just put in the hours and walk away."

"You don't have to convince me," Ben said. "I completely agree with you, and that's really what I want to talk to you about. Irma asked me if I thought there was any possible way I could talk Colin into letting Danny stay, and I hoped that you could help me."

"Me? I could— I could try," Frankie said. "What would you want me to do?"

"I was hoping you'd go with me to meet with Colin when he arrives to pick up Danny," Ben explained. "I thought if you told him how good Danny was with Dad and explained how that youth-senior pairing program works that he might give some more consideration to what would really help Danny in the long run."

"So, you said Colin will be here in two days?"

"Yes, I know I haven't given you much time to think about it. I would have told you sooner if I'd been able to."

"What about Al? What will he do?"

"I've already made arrangements at the care home," Ben said. "I feel I have to talk to Colin, regardless, and I don't know exactly what time or how long it will take. So, it's better just to have Dad attended to for the day."

Frankie felt a fist of apprehension in her stomach at the thought of facing off with Danny's father. She had only met him briefly, and she had not liked the vibe she got from him at all. She was very doubtful that he was a man who could be swayed to change his mind.

Then she thought of the restraint chair and what it must be costing Ben to risk leaving his dad again. He already had so much to deal with, and yet he was willing to try to help someone else. Besides, he was looking at her with those dark blue eyes, which held a question and, suddenly, Frankie had the most peculiar feeling that he was asking if she would stand by him for more than just this.

"Okay, I'll go with you," she said.

Ben's face lit up and he squeezed Frankie's hand.

"We can do this," he said. "We're a team."

His hands felt wonderfully warm and reassuring, and his words sounded in Frankie's ears like a promise.

# Chapter Twenty-One

A flurry of phone calls ensued the following day and Irma reported that eventually Colin had agreed to sit down and talk with them.

"Although," Irma confessed fretfully, "he can be the type that finds it amusing to let you present your whole case before he says no."

Ben decided that Frankie did not need to hear that particular piece of information. She had been apprehensive enough, and he was grateful she had agreed to be there with him. The truth was, he was having a more and more difficult time imagining that the summer would end and he wouldn't see her again.

*There has to be some way we can work it out, Lord. I can no longer pretend to accept that You brought this wonderful woman into my life without a purpose.*

He resolved that as soon as things were settled with Danny he would have a long, honest talk with Frankie and they would figure out if they had something—anything—worth pursuing. Despite the upcoming meeting with Colin, for the first time in a long time, Ben felt a lilt of hope in his heart—like maybe it really could be possible to be a good son and caregiver, and to have someone special in his life, too.

For the first time, he treaded at the edge of forgiving himself.

They had agreed to meet at Irma's at eleven in the morning because Ben thought that dropping off his dad would go more smoothly if he did it on his own. He also thought he could keep the emotional rough spots at bay better without Frankie's perceptive and sympathetic gaze on him.

"Okay," Frankie agreed. "But please don't be late. I have absolutely no desire to face Danny's father on my own."

"I'll be there," Ben promised. "I won't leave you on your own." As he said the words, it suddenly felt like he was talking about more than this particular circumstance. He wondered if Frankie heard their import, too. For good measure, he leaned in and kissed her cheek, breathing in her vanilla-and-peppermint scent, then sat back to enjoy the slow flush of color blossoming on her face.

He was halfway to Irma's when his cell phone rang. He pulled over and looked at it, and was puzzled when he saw that it was the care facility calling. The drop-off had gone remarkably well, for which he had thanked God. He answered with the slightest degree of impatience. He didn't want to be late and cause Frankie to worry, and he hoped it was something simple like his dad asking for his shells or something.

"Hello?" he answered.

"Um… Mr. Cedar?" He didn't recognize the voice, which sounded young and very upset.

"Yes?" he asked, as nerves began to flare in his stomach.

"I— We— I'm sorry to inform you that we don't know where your father is."

Ben's hand clenched around the phone. He felt light-headed, a strange detachment like he was outside himself observing the conversation.

"What do you mean that you don't know where my father is?" The voice asking the question sounded only vaguely like his. "I dropped him off not more than five minutes ago."

There was a pause and then the older, brisker voice of the head administrator came on the phone.

"That's fine, Phoebe," Ben heard her say. "I'll take it from here. Phoebe is new," she explained to Ben, "but she insisted that she be the one to call you since she feels that what happened was her fault."

"What exactly did happen?" Ben didn't even know that his own voice could be so cold. Each second that ticked away while he sought their explanation was one more second that he didn't know where his father was.

He shut his eyes against the troublesome pictures that rushed in and a headache began its assault.

It turned out that Phoebe had thought Al needed a trip to the washroom before taking him into the common room for a snack and games. He had been so docile that she hadn't thought she needed extra assistance. The closest washroom was near an exit. After that, it was easy enough to piece together what had happened. Al, not so docile after all, had shoved Phoebe aside and escaped through the exit. By the time she had recovered herself enough to call someone, he was long gone.

"We are so very sorry, Ben," the administrator said. "I want you to know that we have several staff members out looking for your father and we will alert the authorities if necessary."

Ben heard himself thanking her, and then he clicked off his phone. He tried to pray about what he should do next, but his thoughts were muddled and the words would not come.

He thought maybe his dad would try to find his way back to their cabin, so he began to drive in that direction. He was unable to help himself from imagining all kinds of unfortunate scenarios. Already Al had shoved someone and it was likely that he was very agitated by this time. Who knew how he would react to anyone approaching him, what he might do?

His father wasn't back at the cabin, and with increased anxiety, Ben dashed over to check the Ice Cream Adventure. After that, although he thought it was likely futile, he hurriedly stuck his head into every shop, quickly asking if anyone had seen Al, and leaving almost before they could answer no. He also checked the Nature Center and the library, where the sight of the back of Rae's head shot a bullet of guilt through him. But he didn't have time to think about that now.

Finally, almost sick with worry, he had headed down to the beach, to the water. He didn't think his dad would go near the water because he seemed to be afraid of it, but he didn't know where else to look.

He spotted Al, ambling, stumbling a bit on the beach. He clutched an assortment of things he had picked up—a deflated red balloon, more rocks and shells and a grimy-looking newspaper.

"Dad!" Ben flew to him.

"Hi," Al said.

"Never mind, hi. Let's get you back." Ben eased the "treasures" from his father's grasp and guided him in the direction of their cabin.

Somewhere in the back of his mind he thought he should probably thank God that he had found his father and that he was safe. But, somehow, he just didn't want to.

The discordant background music that had played in his mind through his entire search now leaped to the forefront. Frankie had waited for him and he hadn't shown up. There was absolutely no doubt in his mind about the impact that would have on her.

Then again, he thought, perhaps it was better this way. Perhaps it was better for them both to know now, before he allowed himself to continue with the witless thought that he could have it all. He had met a woman who had stirred emotions in him, and he had let those emotions convince him that he could do it all. He could give his father the care he needed and he could love a beautiful woman.

Because he did love her. Not that it mattered, not anymore. Today had presented him with one of those hard but necessary lessons: he couldn't do it all, and he couldn't have it all. He knew because of the person that he was that he couldn't fail in his responsibilities to his father and live with himself. He would let Frankie go. For her sake, and because it was the only feasible path to take, he would let her go. He didn't deserve happiness. He had made bad choices. He hadn't been there for his mother when she had needed him and now he wouldn't be there for Frankie. He would never have forgiveness, and that's what he had to live with.

Back at the cabin, Ben went through the rote actions of pouring his dad a glass of milk and getting out some washcloths for him.

Then he opened their suitcases. He sat looking at them for the longest time, but they could not answer his question of whether it would hurt more to say goodbye to Frankie and Rae before they left, or not to say it.

If Frankie had been forced to find something to be thankful for during what felt like the longest hour of her life, the only thing she could come up with was that, for Rae's sake, she'd had plenty of practice in keeping her emotions under control and presenting a confident, in-control exterior at those times when she really just wanted to curl up into a little ball and melt.

"I don't think your friend is coming," Colin had said after they had waited for half an hour. Irma wrung her hands and let the teakettle whistle shrilly without going to unplug it. Frankie had thought she would pop out her cheekbones because she was clenching her teeth so hard.

"I'm sure he'll be here," she had said with a bright, brittle note in her voice that she didn't think even sounded like her. "He had to drop his father off."

Inside she agonized that something might have gone wrong; in fact, she was sure it must have. She knew she should probably call the home to find out, but she felt frozen by Colin's judging eyes on her and by her own emotions. She could reason with herself that Ben would have been there if he could have, but, to her heart that was sick with disappointment and worry, it didn't make any difference. No matter what, it seemed she was destined to end up right back where she'd started: facing life on her own and trying to make the best of it.

*It wouldn't hurt quite so much, Lord, if I hadn't started to believe that maybe I wasn't meant to be alone after all.*

She was sure that Ben would explain and be sorry. But, ultimately, she felt that there would always be a reason he couldn't really be there for her, even if he wanted to be. There wasn't any sense getting further involved or exposing Rae to more. The conversation she had planned to have with him, the questions she planned to ask, had proved to be unnecessary.

"So, what now?" Colin asked. "Do you have something you want to say to me or should I just get Danny—or what?"

Irma had finally poured the tea, and in between pushing sips past the lump in her throat, Frankie quickly and nervously ran down the reasons it would be good for Danny to stay put and finish what he'd started.

"I guess I'll think about it," Colin said when she was finished. He added gruffly, "I'm not making any promises, but I do appreciate your interest in my son."

It was a brief, unexpected light to penetrate Frankie's dark mood, but she clung to it and thought of the scripture she had read that morning about God working all things for good for the people who loved Him.

She thought she had prepared herself, but still the sight of Ben sitting on his deck when she returned to the cabin and the way his head reared up when he heard the car tore at her heart.

He looked ten years older, and guilt and trepidation ravaged his handsome features.

"Frankie," he said. "I'm so sorry. I did my best to be there. I *wanted* to be there."

"That's fine," Frankie replied, hearing her

voice return to the distancing briskness she had used with people since her divorce. "I talked to Colin and he said he would think about it. I guess we can't ask for more than that." She paused and her question was softened by genuine concern. "Is your dad okay?"

"Yes, he's fine."

"Well, okay then. That's good." She turned to go into her cabin.

"Frankie, please, we need to talk about this." The plea in Ben's voice halted her footsteps. "Please come and sit down," he said. "I want to at least explain to you what happened."

She turned back very slowly. She owed him at least that much, an inner voice prompted. All right, she would listen. But she wouldn't get drawn into his weary eyes as he spoke.

They both sat stiffly in the chairs. Ben studied his hands, while Frankie gazed off at some unknown distant point.

"I dropped Dad off at the care center," he began. "And it all went very smoothly. I should have known then it was too good to be true."

He looked at Frankie, and she willed herself to be strong and to listen as objectively as possible.

"I was on my way to Irma's," he continued, "when they called and said that Dad had escaped and they didn't know where he was."

Despite her best efforts, a gasp escaped Frankie.

Ben nodded, understanding perfectly her reaction.

"Yeah, as you can imagine, I was pretty much out of my mind with worry. I ran around town looking for him and I finally found him walking on the beach."

"Oh, Ben…"

His mouth collapsed briefly before he steadied it into a fierce, straight line. He looked her in the eyes then, and Frankie could see the will it took to do that.

"There's something else," he said.

"What?"

"Before this happened… Frankie, I was going to tell you that I've grown to care for you. I do care for you. I had let myself begin to hope that we could continue to get to know one another after summer ended. But I know now it's not meant to be. I won't be able to be the kind of man I know you need because my time and attention will always be torn. I—I also plan on ending our time here early, but I couldn't bring myself to do that without at least saying goodbye."

Words teetered on Frankie's tongue, words that wanted to tell him she, too, had developed feelings and had wanted to continue to develop their relationship, but after what Ben had just said, what was the point?

So, all she asked was, "Is it okay if I bring Rae over to say goodbye to Al before you leave? I know she would appreciate being able to do that."

"Yes, please do."

They sat then in silence, as there didn't seem to be anything else to be said. The birds continued their unmindful, happy chatter around them while Frankie's heart tried to resurrect its walls.

# Chapter Twenty-Two

In some ways, Ben thought, it was a relief to have the decision made. They would return to Saskatoon. He would get his father admitted into the best care home possible and he would settle into the life he was meant to live, filled with hard work and dedication to his father's well-being.

Seconds later a collage of memories of Frankie—feisty, smiling, determined, soft— told him that he was only fooling himself.

*Please, Lord, if there's any way, any way at all, that You can give me a different answer and allow Frankie to be part of my life, please show me.*

But if God was answering, He was doing it so quietly that Ben couldn't hear Him.

His father had been docile since his spontaneous excursion, almost as if he sensed that he'd caused great upheaval. He was preoccupied by a picture that Rae had made for him, poking at it and mumbling under his breath. He was quiet enough, at least, so that Ben could continue to prepare the cabin for departure. But it was his own thoughts that kept stalling his hands above half-folded shirts and half-emptied cupboards. Was he giving up too easily? Could they figure out a way? But each time he tried to consider options, he could recall only the feelings of panic and defeat as he frantically searched for his father, all the while knowing in the back of his mind that he had let Frankie down.

"Tree," Al said, and jabbed at the picture. "Tree…this one!" His voice rose.

"Yes, Dad, that's a nice tree," Ben responded automatically and started to pair up socks.

Al mumbled and stuck out his bottom lip.

Ben's cell phone rang and briefly—inexplicably, because there'd be no reason for her to call—he hoped that it was Frankie.

He answered, "Hello, Irma."

"Ben? Where were you today? We were concerned. Is everything all right?"

He battled down a sigh. "There was a mishap with Dad, but thankfully it had a happy ending. I'm sorry I couldn't make it today. I appreciate you checking in."

"I didn't just phone for that," Irma said. "I

don't have Frankie's number, but there's something I hoped you could pass on to her."

"What's that?" Ben felt slightly wary.

"Well, first off I'd better just get it right out in the open that Colin wouldn't let Danny stay."

Another blow, but Ben was feeling unfortunately resigned to them by now.

"There is also some good news," Irma continued. "Frankie spoke about a volunteer program they have where she works, one where they pair up youths and seniors?"

"Yes, she talked about that with me, too," Ben said.

"Well, Colin actually thought it sounded like an idea with a lot of potential, and he's going to speak with some of his contacts in the health sector. He may even consider letting Danny get involved in something like that to meet his community hours."

So, there were still some small blessings but his *thank You, Lord* felt like it stuck a little in his throat.

After Ben had concluded the phone call with Irma, he looked out the window and then opened the front door, hoping he would see Frankie on her deck. But their cabin looked tightly closed up, with no signs of life and, despite hearing some encouraging news from Irma, sadness again threatened to overtake him.

*God*, he prayed. *I know I've let a lot of people down in my life and it feels right now like that's what I'm destined to do. I left Dad to deal with Mom's cancer and I didn't even make it home to say goodbye. Now, I've fallen in love with a wonderful woman and already I've disappointed her. I know I have, even if she says she understands the reasons. Your word talks about forgiveness, Lord. But how can I ever know that my father has forgiven me? And how can I ever forgive myself?*

"Tree! Look!" Al said.

Ben looked out the window again and hoped for an answer, but it wasn't there.

"Yes, Dad," he said again. "Rae drew you a nice picture of trees."

Frankie spent the day walking and thinking. She had found that she couldn't stand the thought of staying in her cabin knowing that Ben was across the way getting ready to leave. Off and on in her head, she tried to practice how she would tell Rae, and concluded again that a straightforward approach was best and that Rae would cope the way she always had. She was truly grateful for the emotional healing that God had brought into her daughter's life this summer, and she prayed it would continue.

She also thanked God for the healing He had brought into her own life, and, although she was hurt over Ben's decision, she found herself thinking of all the ways that he had helped her and Rae and been there for them over the summer. To her surprise, she found herself not dwelling on her own disappointment as much as trying to think of a way to help soothe the pain that Ben carried within him.

*Is this what it means to love again, Lord? To put the needs of someone else above my own? Your word says that there is more joy in giving than there is in receiving, but how? How can I get through to him?*

But the biggest question of all was if she was willing to risk her heart again to do so.

At the scheduled time she met Rae at the library and as they walked slowly back to the cabins, she told her about what had happened with Al that day and how Ben felt that he had to take his dad home.

Rae was pensive. "They won't leave without saying goodbye, right?"

"No, they especially want to say goodbye to you."

They ate what they called "breakfast for supper," which was one of Rae's favourites, but she was very subdued and didn't even ask for more syrup to dip her bacon in.

"Can we go now?" she asked as soon as they were done eating. "Please, can the dishes just wait?"

"We might as well," Frankie said.

She was wrought with nerves and emotion as they tapped on the cabin door, and when Ben swung it open, his face seemed to reflect her feelings.

Rae glanced at Ben with an unreadable face and made a beeline to Al and his picture.

"Will you sit?" Ben asked, sounding like his throat hurt.

Frankie sat.

"Coffee? Or anything?" he asked.

"No, thank you, we just had supper."

Frankie gripped the sides of her chair. If they were going to part ways on such a formal note, she didn't know how she'd be able to live with it.

"I've been thinking all day," she blurted out. "I've hardly done anything but walk around and think, and I know I care for you, too. I just don't know if there's any point to it."

Hope and defeat wrestled on Ben's face. "You care for me?" Then defeat won out. "But it doesn't change anything. Maybe if I knew Dad had forgiven me, I could forgive myself, but, as it is, I just don't know what to do other than to keep doing what I'm doing. It wouldn't be fair to you, or to Rae."

*Lord, help me find the words*, Frankie prayed almost desperately. *Help me to give the right answer.*

"Mom, come look," Rae said. "Al loves the picture I gave to him."

"That's great, Sweet Pea. It's a really great picture."

"He likes the trees," Ben said. "He keeps talking about them."

"I think he really wants you to come and look, Mom," Rae said. "He keeps pointing at one of the trees."

Slowly Al raised his head from the picture and looked directly at Frankie. And, in one of those rare, inexplicable times of clarity, the fog of the disease fell away and his eyes probed hers directly.

"He loves…" Al said. "I loved…" Then his face clouded over once more, and he began to pat the picture again.

Frankie's heart sped up. From the look on Ben's face, she could tell he had noticed the brief, strange connection, too. He went and peered over his father's shoulder to see exactly what he was looking at.

"So, that's why he keeps talking about the tree," Ben murmured. "I'd almost forgotten that Dad proposed to Mom here at Silver Lake, under a tree. It's a big part of our family lore.

You know…" he said, as if a thought was slowly dawning, "even if they'd known what was coming their way, I don't think they would have traded a second of the time they had together."

Suddenly, Frankie knew what to say to him.

"You can know that your father forgives you, Ben," she declared. "You *do* know it."

"I do? How can I?"

"Because you know what the Bible says about forgiveness, and you know the man your father was and what the Bible meant to him. Think about it, Ben! You know, if you just stop being angry with yourself for a moment and really think about it, you already know the answer."

Ben's hands gripped hers and he sought her eyes for answers.

"I don't want to give up on us, Frankie," he said. She watched as her words caused his face to strengthen with new resolve. "I really don't."

Frankie thought about all the things that God had taught her this summer. Now it was clear that the greatest lesson of all was that there was no love without risk.

"Then don't give up," she said. "I don't want to give up, either. We can help each other and God will help us both. Besides, I want to hear the story of the proposal under the tree."

Ben's face lit with surprise and renewed hope and what she wholly trusted was love.

"You would?" he asked.

"Of course," Frankie said. "Since I'm falling in love with you, I'd like to know more of your family history."

"I love you, too, Frankie."

His voice was a whisper that held a thousand wishes and promises.

## Epilogue

Frankie stood at the back of the church at Camp Kindle. Her hands smoothed her ivory silk wedding dress. Its lines were simple and elegant. Silk rosebuds, the peachy-pink color of the sky at dawn, adorned the narrow shoulder straps, with a slightly larger one at her waist.

Eleven-year-old Rae twirled, making the skirt of her light purple dress flare out. She had grown two inches in the last year and had surrendered her braids to a shoulder-length bob that swayed and bounced when she walked.

Frankie's eyes misted at the thought of how Rae was growing up. Then again it didn't take much to fill her eyes with happy tears these days.

It had been quite a year: a year of moves, as Ben and Al came to live in Regina. A year of adjustments, some very painful and difficult, like getting Al settled into the care home where Frankie worked; some painful in a different way, as Rae came to accept Ben as a permanent part of their lives. A year of new challenges, as Frankie enrolled in her nursing classes, and a year of accomplishments, as Danny sent emails to update them on how he was doing and how much he liked visiting the seniors in the Saskatoon nursing homes.

And, through it all, with God's help, she and Ben had learned that they didn't have to be ashamed of their weaknesses, which could turn into strengths when they faced them together and supported each other. And when they relied on God's unending strength.

"Doesn't Al look nice?" Rae whispered. "I tied his bow tie for him." She scanned the guests and announced, "I see Danny."

Then the melodic strains of music began. Rae gave a happy little gasp and smoothed her dress. Frankie took her father's arm and prepared to marry her best friend. She felt like she was going to float away with love and joy. Her heart swelled with a deep thankfulness to God, who had taken what they felt would drive them apart and redesigned it to bring them together.

When she reached Ben, she took his dear, warm, familiar hand and saw all the love and promises he held in his eyes and answered back with her own. And, as they said their vows, she thought of all the challenges they would face with God's help and of all the rewards they would reap—together.

\* \* \* \* \*

*If you enjoyed INSTANT FAMILY,*
*look for these other emotionally gripping*
*and wonderful stories*

*SECOND CHANCE RANCHER*
*by Brenda Minton*
*THE BACHELOR'S UNEXPECTED FAMILY*
*by Lisa Carter*
*A BABY FOR THE DOCTOR*
*by Stephanie Dees*

*Available now from Love Inspired!*

*Find more great reads at*
*www.LoveInspired.com*

Dear Reader,

I'm so excited to share my debut novel with you! Thank you for coming on this journey with Ben and Frankie.

It meant a lot to me to write this book for a few different reasons. My father suffered with Alzheimer's disease before he passed away and, like Ben says, I missed the person he had been long before he actually died. He wasn't a pastor like Ben's father, but was a journalist who taught me my love of books and writing and always encouraged me to write. Many of Al's behaviors are modeled on my dad's, but I know that it's a complex disease that can affect people in many different ways.

I am also a single mom like Frankie—my husband passed away of heart disease several years ago. In writing about Ben, I thought about my husband's kind heart, sense of humor and work ethic.

More than anything, though, I wanted to write a book about second chances. Of course, I thought a great deal about my dad and my husband, and sometimes had a few tears, but more than anything I thought of the many blessings that I've been given as life has continued on—my daughter, my family, my friends, my writing community and, now, readers like you.

Life has unexpected turns, but I believe in God and I still believe in happy endings!

I'm active on social media. Find me on Twitter at @gartshoredonna and on Facebook at facebook.com/dlgartshore. Feel free to email me at deelynn1000@hotmail.com. Come find me—I love to talk about books and writing and hear what people's goals and dreams are.

Thanks again!
*Donna*

# Get 2 Free Books,
## Plus 2 Free Gifts—
### just for trying the Reader Service!

**YES!** Please send me 2 FREE Love Inspired® Suspense novels and my 2 FREE mystery gifts (gifts are worth about $10 retail). After receiving them, if I don't wish to receive any more books, I can return the shipping statement marked "cancel." If I don't cancel, I will receive 4 brand-new novels every month and be billed just $5.24 each for the regular-print edition or $5.74 each for the larger-print edition in the U.S., or $5.74 each for the regular-print edition or $6.24 each for the larger-print edition in Canada. That's a savings of at least 13% off the cover price. It's quite a bargain! Shipping and handling is just 50¢ per book in the U.S. and 75¢ per book in Canada*. I understand that accepting the 2 free books and gifts places me under no obligation to buy anything. I can always return a shipment and cancel at any time. The free books and gifts are mine to keep no matter what I decide.

Please check one: ☐ Love Inspired Suspense Regular-Print    ☐ Love Inspired Suspense Larger-Print
                         (153/353 IDN GMWT)                              (107/307 IDN GMWT)

Name _____ (PLEASE PRINT) _____

Address _____ Apt. # _____

City _____ State/Prov. _____ Zip/Postal Code _____

Signature (if under 18, a parent or guardian must sign) _____

## Mail to the **Reader Service:**
**IN U.S.A.:** P.O. Box 1341, Buffalo, NY 14240-8531
**IN CANADA:** P.O. Box 603, Fort Erie, Ontario L2A 5X3

**Want to try two free books from another line?**
**Call 1-800-873-8635 or visit www.ReaderService.com.**

* Terms and prices subject to change without notice. Prices do not include applicable taxes. Sales tax applicable in N.Y. Canadian residents will be charged applicable taxes. Offer not valid in Quebec. This offer is limited to one order per household. Books received may not be as shown. Not valid for current subscribers to Love Inspired Suspense books. All orders subject to approval. Credit or debit balances in a customer's account(s) may be offset by any other outstanding balance owed by or to the customer. Please allow 4 to 6 weeks for delivery. Offer available while quantities last.

**Your Privacy**—The Reader Service is committed to protecting your privacy. Our Privacy Policy is available online at www.ReaderService.com or upon request from the Reader Service.

We make a portion of our mailing list available to reputable third parties that offer products we believe may interest you. If you prefer that we not exchange your name with third parties, or if you wish to clarify or modify your communication preferences, please visit us at www.ReaderService.com/consumerchoice or write to us at Reader Service Preference Service, P.O. Box 9062, Buffalo, NY 14240-9062. Include your complete name and address.

LIS17R3

# Get 2 Free Books,
## Plus 2 Free Gifts —
### just for trying the
### Reader Service!